D1261344

helen cavanagh

the last piper

For David,
who said the night,
word to bring the Piper
to life — and the word was:
REWRITE!
Thanks for being there,
Helen Cavanagh
Edgars 97

simon & schuster books for young readers

*FOR MY DEAR GRANDDAUGHTERS,
CAITLIN JEAN CAVANAGH AND LAUREN ELIZABETH
CAVANAGH; AND FOR MICHAEL "MIKEY" SORIANO,
WHO WAITED LONG ENOUGH FOR HIS BOOK.*

SIMON & SCHUSTER BOOKS FOR YOUNG READERS
An imprint of Simon & Schuster Children's Publishing Division
1230 Avenue of the Americas, New York, New York 10020

Copyright © 1996 by Helen Cavanagh

All rights reserved including the right of reproduction in whole
or in part in any form.
SIMON & SCHUSTER BOOKS FOR YOUNG READERS
is a trademark of Simon & Schuster.

Book design by Anahid Hamparian

The text for this book is set in 11-point Dutch 809

Printed and bound in the United States of America
First Edition
10 9 8 7 6 5 4 3 2 1

Library of Congress Cataloging-in-Publication Data
Cavanagh, Helen.
The last piper / by Helen Cavanagh. — 1st ed.
p.   cm.
Summary: During a family trip to Scotland, thirteen-year-old Christie becomes
convinced that her asthmatic younger brother is the reincarnation of a Scotsman
who was hanged fifty years earlier.
ISBN 0-689-80481-4
[1. Reincarnation—Fiction. 2. Death—Fiction. 3. Scotland—Fiction.]
I. Title.
PZ7.C2774Las 1996
[Fic]—dc20 95-44423

✢ author's note ✢

Readers ask how I came to write *The Last Piper*.

The story began with a dream, I tell them. In the first dream, a small boy's voice informed me, "My name is Firth Lauder. I lived in Scotland. Before I was borned to Mommy, I gotted hanged to death!"

More dreams followed, and the boy provided me with further details: the hill country, the moor, the half-dead tree, "Em," and the six-toed cat. And the name *Calinda*.

Readers also ask if, in order to write this book, I had to travel to Scotland, to Edinburgh, and the Borders.

One answer I give is, "No, I've never visited Scotland, but I wanted to and still want to very much."

Another answer though, to me equally as truthful, is, "No, I haven't been to Scotland, not in this life anyway. But I hope to go soon. Again."

My sincere thanks for support, encouragement, and information goes to Terry and Mae Mitchell of Glasgow, Scotland; Lily and Brian Gallagher of Spotswood, New Jersey; "Scottie" of East Brunswick, New Jersey, and Edinburgh, Scotland; and Linda and Curt Gillespie of Marco Island, Florida.

I hold that when a person dies,
His soul returns again to earth,
Arrayed in some new flesh-disguise;
Another mother gives him birth.
With sturdier limbs and
     brighter brain,
The old soul takes the road
     again.

—Raynor Johnson,
The Imprisoned Splendor

Blaw yer pipes and beat yer drum,
the best of life is yet to come.

—Old Scots Rhyme

✤ one ✤

"KNOW WHAT, CHRISTIE?"

"What, Mikey?"

"When I was bigger, I lived here."

Sleepy as I was, I had to smile. "Doesn't work that way, peanut. One, we've never been in Scotland before—you know that. Two, no one is bigger before they're little. Other way around, Mikey, little to big, get it?"

Beside me on the back seat of the rental car my little brother shook his head. "I was all growed up here," he insisted, "really, *really* big."

Mikey is small for five, too skinny, a fragile little guy. The only things big about him are his clear green eyes.

"Yeah? So how big *were* you, Mikey?"

He raised his arms as high as they could reach above his head. "Big like this—bigger than Daddy."

His mention of our father took my smile away. I didn't want to play Mikey's silly game anymore.

If he didn't understand that Daddy's death from a heart attack meant he'd gone from us forever, I *did* understand. It still hurt... hurt terribly.

Every time I thought about my father, or when anyone reminded me, like now, the pain of missing him came back full force.

"Listen," I said, "I'm going back to sleep. Wake me up when Mommy gets to a bed-and-breakfast." I pointed past him toward the car window on his side. "See? Rain's stopped. Look outside—count all the sheep on the hills."

"Okay." Mikey scooted across the seat to press his nose to the window glass. Grateful, I settled back against the seat and closed my eyes again.

"Know what, Christie?"

"What now, Mikey?"

"When I lived here, I was Firth."

"Sure, and I was *second!* Or, maybe I was Mary, Queen of Scots."

During the flight from New York to Scotland, I'd read a magazine article about the young queen. Her life had been tragic. How lonely and miserable she must've been, held prisoner in a place called Fothering Lay for nineteen years, then executed anyway. Reading, I'd felt so sorry for her.

"Before I was born to Mommy—"

"Mikey, come *on!* Where are you getting all this weird stuff?"

He had his face turned in my direction when he said it, but he wasn't actually looking at me. In a way, it was as if Mikey was speaking only to himself. Staring at him, I actually felt a chill.

"And know what? Know what, Christie?" His saying my name made me feel better.

"What, Mikey?"

"After? They put me in the ground like Daddy. I didna like it."

Frightened, I sat forward. "Mom, hear what he's saying back here? Who knows where he's getting all this stuff, but I can't take any more."

My mother glanced over her shoulder at me, but I could tell by her blank expression that she hadn't been paying attention to us. So what else is new, I thought.

"Relax, sweetie," she said, "we'll find a place to stay soon, don't worry and—"

"But, Mom, Mikey said—"

"Mommy, go *there*," Mikey screamed. "*Turn,* Mommy!"

Shocked, I flopped back against the seat. Mikey had never been a screamer or a demander. If anything, he's always been almost too quiet a kid, too *good*.

"Michael Steven, chill out," Mom scolded.

"Turn, Mommy," he wailed, "*please!*"

Bewildered, I looked over Mom's shoulder. Through the windshield, just ahead, I spotted a small road sign. The arrow pointed toward the right.

"Hmmm," she muttered, "exactly where I'm supposed to turn."

"What's going on? Mom, how did he know that?"

My mother shrugged. "Lucky guess?"

I made a face at the back of her head. Beside me, Mikey huddled and sobbed quietly.

"Listen, peanut, stop crying, okay? See, Mommy's turning where you said. In just a few minutes, we'll probably find a great place to stay. All kinds of nice inns around here. Anyway, I bet you're hungry. I am. As soon as Mommy stops at an inn, we'll eat."

Fat tears flowed over his thin little face. Mikey's fists, I noticed, were clenched so tightly, his knuckles had turned white.

"Christie," he sobbed, "I hafta see my castle."

His *castle?*

The right turn off the main road brought us to a narrow lane. Purple, pink, and white flowers and shiny green vines draped the rough stone walls on either side of us.

"So beautiful!" my mother exclaimed. "Michael, honey, I'm delighted you spoke up. Let's take a photo."

I was about to reach for Mikey's hand, but he grabbed my hand first and held it tightly.

"There," he gasped, "there it is, Christie."

Sure enough, at the far end of the walled lane stood a smallish stone castle, a castle with everything—turrets, towers, skinny, deep-set windows, a massive front door.

"Look at that," Mom said, "a mini-castle. Michael, after I park, want me to take your picture in front of your castle?"

But when she stopped the car and parked some distance from the castle, she discovered she'd used up all the film. While she stayed in the car to reload her camera, Mikey and I got out. He walked ahead, but I lingered near the car, not sure what I should do.

From where I stood, the castle looked ancient, many of its stones smoke-stained, tumbledown, not in the greatest shape. Still, I figured someone had to live in it. The flower beds that bordered the stone path to the front entrance and the shrubs across the front of the castle were neatly trimmed. I only hoped whoever lived here wouldn't come out and yell at us for taking pictures without permission on their property.

Or, I wondered, did my jittery feelings have to do with the weird things Mikey had said and how he'd acted?

A few feet from me, my brother stood statue-still. For another minute, I watched as he gaped up at the steep rocky hill directly behind the castle.

I walked toward him. As I got closer, I saw he trembled all over and tears streamed down his face. I ran the last few steps to gather him up into my arms.

I held Mikey to me and rocked him the way I've held and rocked him since I was eight years old. He'd been born prematurely, only four pounds, with respiratory problems. Mikey had spent the first two weeks of his life in pediatric intensive care. I wasn't even allowed in to see him during that time, so for those two weeks I found it hard to believe I actually had a little brother.

When my parents finally brought Mikey home from the hospital, I took one amazed look at his tiny face and instantly promised myself I'd keep him safe forever after. Right away I became his second mother and have been ever since. In fact, I know I've been more his mother than Mom has ever been. I guess I still like knowing I'm the most important person in his life, but sometimes—lots of times—I've wished I wasn't. I've never had a chance to start my own life. I've never even had time to make friends, not in the neighborhood and not at school.

"Mikey, it's okay," I soothed. "Don't cry, darlin', Christie's here."

But no matter what I did or said to calm him, Mikey squirmed and twisted in my arms. He flung one arm out and pointed toward the hill. "Up there...there...the tree."

He could barely get the words out, he was wheezing so badly.

"What tree, honey?" I squinted at the hill. What

tree could Mikey be talking about? All I could make out from where I stood were rocks, low bushes, and patches of purple flowers.

As he continued to struggle in my arms, I heard the effort he made to release the air trapped in his lungs. Fear prickled through me. Mikey gasped, his chest heaved and the skin of his little face darkened to blue.

I knew from experience how important it was to keep calm. I set him on the grass, then knelt in front of him. "Easy, Mikey, come on, you can do it."

He stared back at me blankly. I caught him in my arms as he pitched forward.

"Mom, *hurry*," I yelled. I couldn't see her. Had she walked back up the lane to take pictures? I called louder, fighting panic.

At a run Mom came around the corner of the stone wall. I stood, relieved to let her take command of the situation. She scooped Mikey into her arms and ran with him to the car. I loped ahead, yanked open the car door, then stood back to let her put him inside.

"His inhaler's in my carry-on bag up front," Mom said. "Watch him while I get it. *Talk to him!*"

Eyes frightened, Mikey stared up at me. I forced a grin. "Mommy's getting your puffer. Just a sec, okay?"

For more than a year, he'd been fine, not a single asthma attack. Before, when he'd suffered through one, what I'd most hated was my own helpless feeling—the same feeling I had now. This attack felt scarier, mainly because we were so far from home and Mikey's regular doctor.

It got even scarier. Mikey gasped and clawed at his neck. He kicked and his features contorted, his face turned a darker blue.

"Run, Christie," Mom ordered, pushing past me to get at Mikey. "Knock on the door. Ask to use the phone. Whoever answers the door, say it's a medical emergency. Hurry!"

I hesitated. What if while I was gone, Mikey got worse? What if I never saw him alive again. What if, like Daddy, he...died.

No! This wasn't the same as when my father died, when I'd missed his last moments on earth. I ran toward the castle, forcing back my memories and my fears. Mikey needed help now.

Before I reached the front door, it opened. A tall gray-haired woman with a velvety gray cat in her arms stood in the doorway.

"What's wrong, lass?" she asked. "Need help, do ye?"

"Please, yes. My little brother's having an asthma attack. We need a doctor, maybe an ambulance. It's a...a medical emergency!"

She frowned and nodded. "Bring the *bairnie* in. I'll ring up Doctor Dalvercroft in the village. Ian will know what's best for the lad."

The look she gave me seemed full of concern while at the same time she appeared to be studying me carefully. "Go tell your *mother*—bring the lad inside."

The old woman turned from the doorway and disappeared from my sight. My heart pounded. Should I follow her inside? Did she understand that I'd been talking about a matter of life or death?

For a few seconds longer I simply stood there, peering past the door at the greenish light beyond it. I wanted to hurry back for Mikey, and, at the same time, I wanted to run back to Mom and beg her to drive us away from this place.

Stupid, I thought, what am I wasting time for? Mikey needs a doctor!

Over my shoulder I caught sight of my mother walking toward me, Mikey in her arms. His little body looked so limp. As my mother walked, his head lolled and bounced against her shoulder as if—

"Mom," I called out, "is he okay?"

Her widest, most reassuring grin was definitely not what I expected. "Stop worrying, Christie," she said, "he's much, much better. In fact—" She bent her blonde head to plant a kiss on Mikey's cheek, "he's *fine!*"

"Don't ask me how, or why, but from one minute to the next, your brother calmed himself and began breathing normally. Beats me, sweetie."

I realized I'd been holding my own breath as she spoke. I let it out with a loud whoosh. "Thank God," I whispered.

The gray-haired woman reappeared in the doorway. "I've rung up the doctor, he's on the line and he wants me to ask—"

She peered at my mother. "By the size of that smile, missus, I'd surmise the lad's recovered? Good!"

With her free hand she waved us all closer. "Come in, come in, put the bairnie on the couch for a wee nap. Soon as I let the doctor off the hook, I'll make us some tea. A bite to eat?"

Mom kept her smile on as she carried Mikey to the door. "Thank you. Tea sounds wonderful. You're very kind."

The old woman beamed, and, I swear, the cat she still held in her arms smiled right along with her.

"Welcome to Castle Lauder," she sighed, "such as it

stands, worse for wear. I'm Emma Lauder."

"I'm Julia Malcolm," my mother replied, "and my daughter, Christie, and this worn-out little guy is Michael—Mikey."

Mom stopped in the doorway. "You say I can put him down for a nap? Exactly what he needs right now. Oh, and please thank your doctor friend."

As my mother spoke, Mikey lifted his head from her shoulder. As if he were waking from a dream, he blinked, rubbed at his eyes, then looked past Mom's shoulder at the old woman in the castle doorway.

I saw his green eyes brighten. I saw him stretch out an arm toward her. I watched—shocked—as Mikey's small, frail hand reached out to pat the old woman's ruddy, wrinkled cheek. I couldn't believe my shy little brother could've actually done that.

"Hi," he whispered.

Mikey lowered the same hand until it rested squarely on the cat's broad gray velvet head. "Hi, cat," he said softly.

He drew back his hand and laid it against his own cheek, and closed his eyes.

"Home," he said in a clear, much stronger voice, before he put his head back on Mom's shoulder.

Mom didn't say anything and I didn't either. What could we say?

✦ two ✦

EMMA LAUDER DIDN'T APPEAR to mind Mikey's pat on her cheek. Instead, I could tell he'd already won her heart.

In a matter of minutes, Mikey fell sound asleep on the parlor couch. Propped up and surrounded by plump pillows, with a pretty paisley shawl tucked around him, he breathed easily and peacefully. The cat slept too, a soft gray circle at Mikey's feet.

I had no choice then except to follow behind my mother as the old woman led us to her kitchen. Glum and silent I sat at her table, sipped tea and prayed that my little brother wouldn't sleep long so we could leave this place and continue on our way.

For something to do, I watched the clock on the opposite wall. The minutes ticked by, a half hour became an hour.

"Another cuppa tea, Julia?" Emma Lauder asked. "Another scone, lass?"

As badly as I wanted to leave, I had to admit the hot scones with strawberry jam were excellent. Since Mikey still slept and my mother accepted her offer, I did too.

The kitchen did feel cozy and warm, a good shelter against the driving rain outside. The rain had started only minutes after we'd settled at the round table for tea.

"We should be going along soon," Mom sighed and set the dainty flowered teacup into its matching saucer. "I admit to being nervous on these unfamiliar roads in the rain. By the way, how far is Oxton from here, Mrs. Lauder?"

"Never was wed, so it's Ms., as they say. I prefer Em." She winked at me. "Short and to the point and, even spelled backwards, it's still *Me!*"

My mother laughed and I managed a half-smile.

"Oxton? That's where you're headed? Where are you staying in Oxton, if you don't mind a busybody asking?"

"I'm not sure where," my mother explained, "though I'm hoping I won't have to drive much more today. The company I work for—Pennington Textiles— took care of our airfare and actual travel arrangements. I opted to wait until we arrived to find a place to stay. I thought it'd be fun and much better to have choices.

"A co-worker did provide me with a list of recommended inns and bed-and-breakfasts, or whatever they're called here," Mom explained. "If I have my maps and facts right, two of the best places are in this immediate area."

I sat across from Em. As my mother continued talking, I watched the old woman's expression change from friendly interest to gloom to bright interest again.

"You are right to be worried—thanks be that you stopped here first. Och, doesn't the Lord work His mysterious ways.

"Last of July, and three weeks of August, ye'll be

hard put to find vacancies. The International Festival in Edinburgh, ken? People come for that from near every country in the world. The Borders, close as it is to the grand, gray city, takes in the tourist overflow."

My mother put her head in her hands. "Of course, I've heard about the Festival, but I never thought it would affect us! I should've made reservations ahead, but—Heavens! Now what will we do?"

From under my lashes I studied my mother. I knew something she didn't know I knew. When the opportunity first came up for this business trip overseas, Mom had called Grandma and Pops to ask if they'd keep us for the month. As usual, they said no, they were too busy. But if they'd said yes, Mom would've gladly left us behind.

"Not to worry even a wee bit," Em said. "I have an idea."

I knew then what was on her mind, and it made me nervous all over again. Emma Lauder was nice enough, but we knew nothing about her. Something about her and about the place itself bothered me, though I couldn't have said exactly what.

"What I'm asking Julia," Em said, "would you stay with me? Be my paying guests at Castle Lauder. It seems Providence bought you my way, and—"

She sighed. "The truth is, I could use the cash and the company. Except for my malkin—"

"What's a *malkin*?" I asked.

"A cat, lass." Em shook her head. "This one is Sixtoes, after the extra toes on each paw. Since I was a child, and long before that, the Lauders managed to keep a six-toed cat. As for the name *malkin*—in Scotland, every gray cat is a malkin!

"So, as I was saying, Julia, to be honest, I canna offer you as much as the finer places. Comfy here— though—clean and plenty of room. Castle Lauder isna on the list of recommended B & B's, nor could it be without fixin' up and advertisement. Still, to set yer mind to rest, I'd give ye good local references to my character.

"Aye, for true," she said, "I'd be glad to have you three stay."

The wistfulness I heard in her voice made me realize she had to get lonely sometimes living in this castle all by herself.

"It's wonderful of you to offer," Mom said, as Em refilled her teacup for the third time, "but I'm here on business. Most days I'll need to be off and around the countryside. The places on my list all provided supervision for the kids and I hope—"

"Och, I'd keep the sharpest eye for Christie and Mikey's well-being and safety," Em assured her, "and they'd like it here. So much to do, plenty of land to run and ramble, hills and moors and shady glens."

I listened, becoming more uneasy by the second. Mom sounded as if she might go for what Em offered. But what would I do here for the rest of July and first two weeks of August?

I'd known ahead of time it would be up to me to see to Mikey, entertain him, spend my every waking hour with him.

Nothing new about that, and it didn't do me much good to complain about it. Especially now that Daddy was gone, I was It! More and more, Mom put her business—her career—first!

I'd hoped at least that Oxton was a big enough village to have shops, a movie house, maybe a video arcade.

"In the garden shed, I've got a couple of old bicycles, good enough for knocking around," Em said, "and you two could help me in my garden. I'll teach you all sorts of fascinating lore about my plants and herbs. Ever make berry jam, lass?"

"No, never did," I answered. I tried to catch Mom's eye, but she wouldn't look my way.

"Castle Lauder isn't fancy, far from it. Without the funds to refurbish all these years since...since my family passed on, the castle *is* a wee bit tumble-down, but—"

"Oh, I disagree," Mom said, and I could tell she wasn't saying it to be polite. "Your castle is charming, and I admit it—inspiring. You see, Em, my business in the Borders is to research Tartans and come up with a few designs of my own based on the originals. Pennington Textiles is eager to develop and design a collection of new tartans. I'll need to visit and spend time at a number of old mills, museums, weavers' crofts. How close are you to all of that, Em?"

"You're in luck, Julia. Lauder is central. Right here is the most important museum of the Borders, not to mention Thirlestane Castle. I could put you in touch with a few of the original weavers. Live quite nearby, they do."

Em spoke quickly. "My cooking is plain, but plentiful. In summer I have a gardenful of fresh vegetables and herbs, and, as you may have noticed, I *do* like to bake."

Mom laughed. "Oh, we noticed, didn't we, Christie? Could very well be, the reason I decide to stay here, Em, is because I can't move from this chair."

Em leaned forward across the table. "So you'll stay at Castle Lauder? Aye, and you could each have your own room since you'll be my only guests. Would you like a tower room, Christie? You could have the room I had as a girl."

"About your rates," Mom began, and I knew, for sure, whether I liked it or not, we were staying.

While Em and Mom sat there at the table making financial arrangements, I excused myself, saying I wanted to check on Mikey.

In the parlor, he was still asleep. I plunked myself down in a soft chair on the opposite side of the room so as not to disturb him. Sixtoes opened one eye, studied me for a minute, then jumped down from the couch. The cat strolled toward me and leaped into my lap, did a 360-turn and settled down to sleep again. When I set my hand on its velvet, smoke-colored fur, the cat began to purr loudly.

"What choice do I have, cat?" I whispered. "What choice do I *ever* have?"

"Christie?"

In his nest of pillows on the couch, my brother sat up straight. He looked all around him, his eyes wide. The best words I could think of to describe how he looked to me were "rosy" and "healthy." It struck me as odd, too, that only a short time ago he'd looked so bluish and strained I'd thought he might die.

"How're you doing, Mikey?"

"I'm good," he said. "Christie, Malkin likes you! Malkin doesn't like everyone."

I squinted at him. "Did you hear us talking in the kitchen?" I asked. "Pretty good ears you have, peanut.

Anyway, the cat's name is Sixtoes, not Malkin."

"Sure—six toes," he said. "Extra toes. That's why Malkin's a special cat."

He had to have been listening to the kitchen conversation. I could think of no other explanation.

I shrugged. "Guess he is. Mikey, guess what, we're staying here instead of Oxton."

Instantly, he was off the couch and at my side. "You mean it? Mommy said?"

Gently, he pressed his nose to the sleeping cat's nose. "Told you, Malkin—I'm home."

I groaned. "Mikey, I don't think you should keep saying stuff like that. Em—Ms. Lauder—the lady who lives here, will get upset. Since we're staying, you'd—"

"*Em! Where is she? I really like Em!*"

Startled awake, the cat got up, jumped down, and streaked after Mikey as he headed down the hall toward the castle kitchen. I realized, watching Mikey go, that I hadn't had to tell him where to find her. That made me mad. Why it made me mad, I couldn't explain, but it did.

I sat there, wondering if my mother intended to get around to telling Em how we happened to end up at her castle. That it had been Mikey's idea—his crying and screaming and carrying on—that had brought us down the lane to Castle Lauder.

But if she didn't say anything, I knew Mikey would. I guessed he was doing just that while I sat in this soft, blue chair and worried about it. I got up and followed Mikey and Malkin. Actually, I liked that name better than Sixtoes—Malkin sounded right somehow.

"So you like my cat, too, lad?" Em was saying when I reached the kitchen doorway. "I'll have you know the cat is my closest friend in this old stack o' stones—a faithful companion."

Mikey stood beside her, gazing up into her face. "Remember we used to be closest friends, Em?"

Mom and I exchanged glances. Mom ran both hands through her hair.

"*Used* to be, lad?" Emma smiled. "You say we were friends? Tell me about it."

I felt a strong urge to leave the room.

Mikey's voice sounded wistful. "Don't you know me, Em? I'm Firth. When I was bigger, I mean."

He looked down at himself and sighed. "'Cept I'm not big anymore, right now I'm just this little kid.

"Remember, Em, how strong I was? I threw the caper and tossed the stone, and I could lift you over my head. You'd say, 'Firth, Firth, put me down, I'll tell Mum,' but you would laugh so hard, couldna say nothin' bad about me ever."

Em gasped. "Wait a wee minute, lad, you said— *Firth?* How do you know *that* name?" The color had drained from her face.

"Firth, your *brother!*"

The old woman bowed her head, but not before I saw the tears glinting at the corners of her eyes.

"Mikey, stop," I hissed, "you've made Em cry with all your silly talk."

"I did?" Mikey reached out to touch her face again and when he felt the tears wet his fingers, he looked as if he might burst into tears himself.

"Don't cry, Em, I don't want you to cry." He sidled in closer to put his head on her chest.

"You gotted real old, didn't you, Em? What happened to all your good hair? 'Member how long it was?"

"Michael, that's *enough!*" Mom said, getting up from the table. Her voice came out shaky although I figured she'd wanted it to sound firm.

"Em," she continued, "I apologize for this. I don't know what to make of it myself. In the car, not long before we reached Lauder, Michael—well, said things. He claimed he'd lived here before! Nothing would do but that I drive down your lane. He directed us here!

"To be honest, Em, when I sat your castle at the end of the lane, I couldn't believe my eyes. Mikey got hysterical—he'd told Christie some nonsense about how his name used to be Firth and—well, I don't know what to make of it."

I hid my surprise. My mother had been paying attention in the car, after all.

"He told Christie he'd died. He said, 'Before I was born to Mommy, I died.' Can you imagine? We didn't know what to make of it—or him. He's never acted up like this before, has he, Christie?"

I nodded, glad that she'd thought to ask me. After all, I spent more time with Mikey than she did.

Mom picked up her purse. "We're terribly sorry about this, Em. I'll fully understand if you want to change your mind about us staying with you."

"You'll stay," Em said, pulling a hankie from her dress pocket. She used it to dab at her eyes. "Don't mind me, it's just that hearing him say my dear brother's name…"

My mother's smile was uncertain. A coincidence, of course, I thought. Could it be that Border country doesn't mean only the border lands between Scotland and England, but once we've crossed over a certain

line, everything changes? Could we be in the...
Twilight Zone?

The old woman wiped at her eyes again. "His true
name was Fergus, but I called him Firth and that name
stuck. Aye, a fine big brother. With him came all the
adventure, laughter, and fun I knew as a child." She
sniffled once more, then replaced the hankie in her
pocket.

I left the safety of the doorway, and came to stand
beside her.

"Em," I asked quietly, "are you saying you *did* have
a brother named Firth?"

She nodded, dabbing at her eyes again.

"You mean, Mikey is right? But how could he
know? Mom, how could he? This is *too weird!* It *is*
the Twilight Zone."

"Aye, dearie, t'is true. The lad's right, I did once
have good hair. Not gold, not red, but a mixture of
both. Firth insisted it was topaz! Big and strong and
manly he was, but a gentle artist at heart. Aye, I've
missed him so these many years."

"Maybe," Mom said, "we should change the subject. Or, at least, give it a rest. But I do apologize, Em,
and I—"

Em nodded. "One more question. Tell me, lad,
what's all this about dyin'?"

Mikey nodded solemnly. "I dinna do it, Em. I
dinna!"

A shiver raced along my spine.

Em studied him for a long moment, then sighed. "I
never doubted my brother's innocence all these years.

"Now, tell you what, we'll put this subject on the
back burner with the teakettle."

"Tomorrow, we'll talk and reminisce again, but now it's time for bringing luggage in. You're here to stay for a bit, laddie. And, look from my window...the rain's stopped, and the sun's about to set."

"It's pretty," I said, "but why is it so green out? The air—everything—looks green!"

"Aye, lass, that's the Gloaming. You've heard about the Gloaming?"

I shook my head and headed for the kitchen doorway. I had heard enough weirdness for one day. "I'll get the luggage," I said over my shoulder.

Outside the air felt soft and looked absolutely green. I just stood there beside the rental car for a moment in the soft green gloam.

Standing there I felt more alone than ever, and scared. I felt confused and scared for myself, but mostly for Mikey.

But what could I do except stay and wait for the three weeks of my mother's business trip to pass so we could go home.

Why, though? I wondered. Why had Mikey said those things to Emma Lauder?

Not a new question for me. For the past seven months I'd asked and asked myself the same terrible question—*why?...why?*

✢ thRee ✢

"LIKE IT?" EM ASKED. "I've spent many a happy hour here."

"It's nice," I answered politely, remembering that she'd said this tower room had been hers once.

Em walked over to a tall wooden armoire and opened the doors. "Here's your closet, lass. If you need more hangers, let me know."

She closed the doors to the armoire and gestured at their painted surfaces. "We painted this chest together when we were young, still in our teens. I did the flora and Firth did the fauna and the wee people. Come look."

I couldn't refuse. I walked to where she stood. "What wee people? All I can see are animals, deer, a couple of rabbits, and some birds."

Beside me, Em sighed deeply. "It's over fifty years since Firth's gone, but looking at this bonnie piece, it seems yesterday.

"Aye, my brother had the talent, he did, the art and the music and storytellin'." She turned to look at me. "There's magic in this paint, Christie, only t'is hidden to most who view it, hidden among the leaves and trailin' vines and blossoms."

"Magic?" I couldn't fathom what she meant, and I wasn't sure I wanted to know.

"Squint a slight bit," she urged. "Look deep into the paint."

Whatever Em meant, I couldn't see anything but a pretty garden scene. Then, after a moment, I did! Tucked inside a cup of blue flowers, I saw a tiny, impish face with pointy ears and chin.

Within the folds of a curled green leaf, another little being played a fiddle. From behind a fringe of fern, a dainty miniature lady in a long green gown waved a lavender thistle wand. Inches from her, I discovered another lady, this one wearing a tiny golden crown.

"Oh, *now* I see."

I blinked and discovered four more little people, two with dotted butterfly wings, the other two mounted on the back of a light-brown cricket.

"Best known as the Fairy Folk," Em explained. "Whenever we walked out on the moor, Firth and me, we hoped to meet them." She chuckled, "They never showed their wee, precious selves. I still look for them on the moor whenever I'm out herbing."

I stared at her. "You think fairies are *real*?"

"You don't, Christie?"

I shook my head.

"*Och*, lass, could I tell you stories! Scotland is a magical land, well stocked with invisibles and unexplainables. It's why I love it, I suppose. Where else can a body expect the unexpected at near every turn of the old roads and paths?"

I didn't know what to say, but I did wonder about something she'd mentioned a few moments before. Since she didn't appear to be in any great hurry to leave the room and give me some privacy, I figured I might as well ask.

"Em, you said your brother died more than fifty years ago. How old was he when…when it happened?"

"Twenty-eight," she said, "in his prime. I'd turned twenty-four and was engaged to be married. Firth was betrothed, as well. We thought—"

Em walked past me to kneel on one of the cushioned window seats. She unlatched the long window and pushed. Both sides of the window swung outward. "Leave it open while we're downstairs to freshen the air."

Just like that, she changed the subject. I stood there, waiting for her to answer my question, but the seconds stretched into a minute of silence, and I knew she didn't intend to tell me.

Not that I blamed her too much. I didn't feel angry because I knew only too well how hard it was to talk about someone you loved who'd died. Except the big difference is, I thought, Em's had fifty years to get over it. For me, it had only been seven months since my father's death.

"Come downstairs when you're ready," she told me as she got up from the window seat and headed for the door. "We'll have lots of chances to chat, ken?"

I must've looked confused because she laughed and took time to explain. "*Ken?* is like your *you know?* Here a day or two, and ye'll be saying it yerself, Christie."

"Maybe," I answered as she left the room, my room for the duration.

After she'd gone, I finished unpacking.

On the table beside the double bed, I stacked the new paperbacks I'd brought with me. In the table drawer I put my small tape recorder and the blank book I'd already begun as a special travel journal.

I sat on the side of the bed, took out the journal again, and turned to the first page. This morning in Glasgow, while we waited to board the train for Edinburgh, I'd taken time to write a few lines. I reread the first entry.

We're here! I should be excited, but I'm not. Mom keeps telling me, not every girl my age gets to spend three weeks of summer vacation in Scotland. I would be excited if Daddy were here with us. It doesn't seem right. This trip was his important dream, not Mom's.

When I was little, before Mikey was born, Daddy would hold me on his lap and tell me: "One of these fine days we'll go to Scotland— me, Mommy, and you, my bonnie Christie. We'll head for the Borders, land of our hearts and blood."

Mom would laugh and laugh and say, "Doug, you're an American, remember?"

And Daddy would puff up his chest, pound it, and bellow: "I'm a Malcolm, descendent of a Scots king, and don't ever forget it, woman!"

Sadder than ever, I replaced the journal in the drawer.

I haven't remembered that for years. Funny, this morning I had, word for word. Probably being in Scotland brought back the memories.

Now, sitting on the bed, I couldn't help but wonder what Daddy would've thought and said about Mikey's crazy memories. I had to smile. Knowing my father, he probably would've gotten all enthused. I imagined him laughing, then saying with his usual gusto, "What's strange about it? Not strange at all. What else, Mikey?"

Restless, but not ready to go downstairs, I walked over to the window. I had seen the view from the front window, but not the one from the back. Kneeling on the cushions as Em had done, I took one look and gasped.

I hadn't seen a tree on the hill before, but there it was, its branches gnarled and twisted and leafless. The tree stood alone on the slope. To me, it appeared totally lifeless.

The hill itself was a series of rocky ledges, a narrow path wound upward through clumps of grass and masses of purple flowers. I studied the view carefully. From the front of Castle Lauder, Mikey could not have seen this tree, but he'd mentioned it, trembled because of it, and—he'd been right again!

Higher up the hill, I saw more craggy rocks and patches of gold and green and purple, but the mist, swirling above like white ribbons, hid the top. The hill itself was beautiful, but—I shivered—definitely not the tree. That dead, ugly tree gave me the creeps.

A short time later when I left the tower room and went down the circular stairway, I took my time. Every other step or so, I stopped to study a framed picture, or simply stood still, running my hand over the cool stone walls.

Looking around me, touching the castle wall, made me feel as if I'd walked into a King Arthur movie.

I heard Mom's voice coming from the parlor. I joined her there, surprised to find Mom, Em, and Mikey seated close to each other in a semicircle, their chairs pulled up to a fire blazing in the hearth. A fire in July? Still, it felt good. The castle was chilly.

As soon as Emma spotted me, she got up from her chair. "I'll make a small supper," she said. "Tea and scones canna hold you through the night."

Mom had her work papers spread on her lap. On the floor beside her chair was a map. She gestured toward it. "As it turns out, we're in the ideal spot. The places I'll need to visit are all nearby. Tomorrow, I'll start with Galashiels and check out the old Weavers Corporation. Right now though what I need most is a good night's sleep. Some sleep, and I might even get my head on straight again! What do you think, honey?"

"I think *my* head will never get straight again," I answered. "Mom, how could he—" I glanced over at Mikey who sat petting Malkin and lowered my voice, "— remember about Em's brother? I mean, he's just a little kid. Do you think he really could've lived here before? I've heard about past lives, but how does it work?"

Mom shook her head. "It *doesn't* work. You're talking about reincarnation, sweetie. Although it's only a theory, it's quite fashionable these days. But do *I* think he lived here before? Absolutely not, so don't worry about it."

"But what if it happened the way he says it did? If before he was born to you, he died? Em *did* have a brother named Firth. She told me upstairs Firth died fifty years ago."

Mom put her fingers to her lips. "No more, please. Relax, don't worry about it. You'll see, by morning he'll have forgotten all about it. For now, let's just eat, rest, and make small talk"—she yawned—"extremely small talk!"

At nine o'clock, Mom declared she couldn't keep her eyes open a minute longer. I'd already put Mikey to bed in the room next to Mom's, a room Mikey insisted had been his "old" room. He didn't say any more than that because he fell asleep before I had him in his pajamas.

Later, after saying goodnight to Em, I followed Mom up the stone stairs. When I shut the door behind me in the tower room, I hurried to get undressed. Only after I'd put on my nightgown and crawled beneath the covers, did I think about brushing my teeth.

Skip it, I told myself, thinking about the location of the bathroom down the hall. Instead I sat up in bed with my new journal and a ballpoint pen.

I wanted to write about the day, but after a while I put the book and pen back in the drawer. My mind felt too boggled to put all my thoughts and questions into words.

When I'd turned off the bedside lamp, I thought about closing the window, but the breeze blowing through the round room felt good. I left it as it was. Instead, as I've done every night since January, I thought about Daddy, about death.

Death—what is it? I wondered. Why does it happen? Why my father, just turned forty? Forty isn't really so old, I thought—not like Grandma and Pops.

I longed for sleep to come and take my questions away.

Every night, the same questions! I'd learned to wait, not fight my sad thoughts, until they blurred and drifted enough for sleep to come and help me escape.

Already I felt warm, drowsy, my thoughts were hazy and...

❖ ❖ ❖

The room was dark when I awakened. Huddled beneath the heavy quilt, I should've been warm enough, but I wasn't. My hands and my feet, especially, were freezing.

I'd been dreaming. In my dream I had gone outside, barefooted, in my thin, cotton nightgown determined to climb the hill behind the castle.

Except for silver streaks of moonlight shining through the mist, it was dark, and the path up the hill was narrow and rough, strewn with sharp-edged, slippery stones. I moved upward quickly, my bare feet skimming above the stones.

Now, curled up under the quilt, I remembered why it had seemed so important to get to the top of the hill. I'd heard music—music that called to me—a strange, haunting sort of music.

In the dream, I knew that I would discover the source of the strange music if I could just make it to the top. Once I'd found it, all my questions about death would be answered and I'd never have to worry about it again.

But as I lay in bed, my teeth chattered and my heart pounded as if I'd actually been outside in the chilly darkness in only my nightgown—as if I'd been climbing the steep rocky hill.

A dream, but so real. I couldn't pull myself all the way awake. Part of my struggle to leave my dream behind was that I could still, faintly, hear the music.

Then the reason I was so cold, came to me. I'd left the window wide open. Simple as that. My eyes had adjusted to the darkness of the round room. I got out of bed, hurried across to the back window, and was about to pull both sides inward, when I heard it, really heard it coming to me from the crest of the hill—the music I'd heard in my dream.

I leaned as far out of the window as I dared, straining to see through the mist. After a moment, I did see—was I imagining it?—someone silhouetted against the indigo moonlit sky.

Could it be Em? At night, if she couldn't sleep, did Em climb the hill, I wondered? It could be her, because, outlined against the sky, the figure I saw wore a skirt. The figure also held something bulky—a bag—in its arms.

No, not Em, not a woman, but a man wearing a skirt!

Wait, not a skirt, a *kilt.* Not a bag, *bagpipes!* On the top of the hill was a piper, a lone piper playing music in the middle of the night!

For the longest time I listened and looked. The breeze blowing on me from the window was cold and damp, but I no longer worried.

This is Scotland, I remembered. Why shouldn't a piper from the neighborhood be playing at night? After all, what did I know? If Em didn't mind, why should I mind? Besides, as sad as the music made me feel, I liked it.

And, I thought, standing by the open window, if this is a dream and I'm not awake, so what?

At last, the music died away, and the swirling mist closed over the top of the hill and the kilted figure disappeared from my sight.

The bed was warm when I crawled back into it—warm, as if I'd never left it.

✤ four ✤

"GOOD, YOU'RE UP," MOM said when I arrived in the kitchen the next morning. "I was just on my way to wake you."

Dressed in skirt, blazer, and high heels, with her hair and makeup just so, she already had that look in her eyes. That look meant she had her business plan set for the day, a plan much more important to her than Mikey or me.

Wouldn't it be great, I thought, if my mother wasn't always in such a big hurry? I wanted so much to share the dream I'd had, but I knew she wouldn't want to hang around long enough to hear it. Anyway, even if she did have time to listen, would she be interested? I doubted it.

Interesting to me, though, that dream. I'd stayed in bed long after waking, going over and over it. I'd remembered some of the tune the piper had played and hummed it.

At the kitchen table, Mikey smiled up at me before he lifted a heaping spoonful of something whitish and lumpy to his mouth.

Em stood at the sink, filling the kettle with water. She glanced at me over her shoulder. "Porridge for you, lass, or bannocks? Whatever you like, I'll be glad to cook up."

"What are *bannocks*?"

"Oatcakes, a bit like your pancakes, only—"

"Would you excuse me?" Mom interrupted. "Christie, I need some help carrying my equipment to the car. I'd like to leave now, get an early start."

After Mom kissed Mikey goodbye, I followed her from the kitchen through the parlor to the front door. Her camera bag, portfolio, notebooks, and Daddy's briefcase were piled on the stone floor. Seeing the butter-soft brown leather briefcase made me mad. I wanted it. It should've been mine to keep, but I'd never asked Mom for it. Maybe I'd been afraid she'd say no.

When she was seated in the rental car with all her work stuff arranged on the back seat, Mom looked at me through the rolled-down window. "I'm counting on you today, sweetie," she said as she always did. "Here's a list of the places I'm planning to visit, in case of emergency. Not that I expect any!"

I turned away and began to walk back to the castle. "Okay, Mom. Sure, don't worry about a thing."

Did she ever worry? I wondered angrily. Probably not, and why should she? I stomped up the wide stone steps to the front door. Why should Mom worry, when she had me to worry for her?

As I walked, dread prickled at my neck and shoulders.

"*Wait!*" I ran back to the car. "What if he *does* have another attack?"

"I doubt he will," she said. "Remember, yesterday happened to be Mikey's first long flight, then the train ride and the drive here. He was overtired—all stressed out. Mikey will be just fine today. I'm sure of it."

"See for yourself how contented he looks this morning, Christie. He does love that big ol' cat, doesn't he?"

Mom turned the key in the ignition. The car purred to life. "One thing I do ask. I've already spoken to Em about it. About this past-life fantasy of Mikey's, if he does come out with any more outrageous stuff, I asked her not to encourage him to talk about it. I'm asking you, too."

She made a face. "To think I was actually ready to believe it! I should have known better. We live, we die—that's it. Anything else is wishful thinking. There are no easy answers. None."

She put the car in gear.

"Past life? But—"

"But, nothing, sweetie. This morning Em and I had time to chat before Mikey came downstairs. It turns out that the tragic tale of Em's brother, Firth, is legend around here. Actually, the tale has traveled. It's been written about, published in Edinburgh newspapers and magazines—also in an anthology of Scottish lore. If it's been circulated so widely here, who's to say it wasn't sent over to the United States?"

"Mom, Mikey can't read."

"A video, then."

Mom sounded sure of herself. But I wasn't so sure. Would Mikey have sobbed and trembled and suffered an asthma attack over a video he'd happened to see? Or because he was tired?

"Bye, dear," she said, checking her watch. "I'm off. In case of emergency, just call around, track me down. I won't be that far away. Of course, I had no idea we'd be staying with Em, but her place is ideally situated for me. Great, how things worked out."

I'd already walked away as she talked. Without turning around, I stuck my hand in the air and waved goodbye, just so I wouldn't get accused of rudeness.

Great? Easy for her to say. For me, the day stretched ahead endlessly. What would I do all morning and afternoon? How could I entertain Mikey?

I hurried to join Em and Mikey in the kitchen. On the way I decided I was hungry. Bannocks! I could try them, couldn't I? Better bannocks than porridge.

So Mom had warned Em not to talk about Mikey's "past life"? Why? Because she had done that, more than ever, I wanted to know. I *had* to know!

Luckily, Em was alone in the kitchen. Through the kitchen window above the sink, I spotted Mikey seated on a stone bench in the back garden. Malkin sat beside him, busily licking his paws. I sat down, mentioned bannocks, and while Em stirred up a batter in a pale blue bowl, I asked my first question.

"Em, did your brother become a legend after he died? My mother told me his story got in the newspapers and—"

"Aye, but your mither told me not to talk about it."

"She only said she didn't want us to encourage Mikey, not to discuss it in front of him. She never said we couldn't talk about it, Em—you and me. He can't hear us."

I waited until she served me a plate stacked with three thin steamy oatcakes. She passed me a bowl of cream cheese mixed with marmalade, which she told me to spread on and between the bannocks. I did, took a first bite, and announced, "Delicious!" Em looked pleased.

"Your mither seems to think Mikey must've seen a

video or a television program about Scotland and my brother. She seems to think it explains how Mikey knew about Firth, about this castle and me. What's your opinion, Christie?"

"If Mikey watched any such TV program or a video, I would've watched it too. Wherever he is, I am."

"Oh?" Em asked. "You and the lad are close, I ken, but you two canna be together all the time."

I hadn't intended to do much talking, or to tell her anything personal, but I had to make her understand how it was.

"Yes, we are. Since Mikey was born, he's been more my child than my mother's. See, Mom works all day."

What I could've told Em, but didn't say aloud was: "Then when she comes home from Pennington, she does research or works on her designs until bedtime. She hopes if she makes extra effort she'll get promoted to head designer. Since my father died, Mom has been really pushing to get that promotion. She says we need the money." And probably we did, I thought, but—

"No time for yourself, lass?"

"Not much. Anyway, Mikey does go to preschool, but they don't show videos or watch television there. So I know he couldn't have known about your brother or you."

"How *do* you think he knew about us, Christie?" Em asked seriously. She'd seated herself in the chair across from me, and her faded blue eyes seemed brighter.

"A past life? My mother may not think it's possible. But since I don't know anything about past lives, or how they're supposed to work, I don't have an opinion yet."

"I'm not the one to ask about reincarnation, my

friend. Dr. Dalvercroft is. He lives in Lauder, but he's often very busy, travelin' back and forth to Edinburgh or abroad."

"Could we talk to him?" My fork clattered against the edge of the plate as it fell from my fingers. "Oops, sorry, I chipped your plate."

"Not to mind, dearie," Em said. "A chipped dish will match the rest of the Lauder dishes these days.

"After Firth met his awful fate, our lives and our luck went steadily downhill."

After another glance out the kitchen window to make sure Mikey was safe and sound in the garden, I propped my elbows on the table. I wanted to learn all I could about Em, Firth, and her family. I needed to know. Mikey worried me a lot.

"Fair enough for me to explain about Firth," Em said. "As his only living kin, I can be the expert. As for the other—the reincarnation business—I canna say. We'll wait for Ian to come by, as I know he will. Have your questions ready for the good doctor."

"Thanks, Em, I will."

"After Firth died, our folks, including Uncle Peter who lived with us, did poorly. Och, how we all grieved. As the youngest and strongest, it fell to me to see to things. Mither and Dad and Uncle all died within months of each other, died of shattered hearts and dreams and pride. The man I'd thought to marry tired of all the gloom and death and found himself a cheerier girl to wed.

"Jilted or not, I could've gone on decently enough, but for the dark clouds of scandal. All the whispers about my brother being a thief and murderer."

"*Thief? Murderer?*"

"Och, they'd had to hang him for a reason, lass! Not that he was guilty, mind ye. To my dying day, I'll never believe my brother could steal from us or the Douglases, much less murder his Calinda."

"Who...who was that?" I whispered, not sure I wanted to hear about it. But I'd asked her and—

"His sweetheart, his fiancee, Calinda Douglas," Em said. "They were to marry soon. Then, in the dead of night, a gang of four arrived to drag Firth from his bed. Against his will, they forced him up Lauder Hill, where they hanged him!

"I remember the fearful commotion, how can I not? His protests, Mither's screams, Da's useless pleas to stop them. One of the gang had to knock Uncle Peter unconscious, he fought so.

"My poor, poor brother! Only as the noose tightened, and before he dropped and swung, did Firth learn his darling Calinda was dead. Hidden—cowering!— behind bushes on the hill, I heard them tell him, heard their terrible taunts.

"Calinda's elder brothers *had* to have been three of the hangmen, but I've never guessed the fourth. If only they'd waited for the truth—not been such ragin' hotheads."

Em sighed. "Still, they had to be out of their minds with grief for their little sister. Hard though, from that summer night 'til this day, the Douglas brothers pass me by with nary a word.

"Shouldna complain, dearie. I do the best I'm able under the long, sad circumstances. A few friends and neighbors proved loyal. My cousin Rab stuck by me, at the least. He's dead and buried now, too..."

Across the table, Em dabbed at her watery eyes.

"Sorry," I said. "I shouldn't've asked."

"Not to worry. It's been cruel, it's been hard, with our good name tarnished and family fortune, deeds and documents, silver and valued trinkets never found. But I'm alive, and full of strength and I thank God each day for my blessings.

"I'm past seventy, but I still wonder, even without your inquiries, what my life would've been like had Firth lived to marry Calinda and become the person he was meant to be."

Em smiled tearfully. "Then along comes the Malcolms and my questions are set out in a fresh new light! Not often I get a chance to talk about my brother, and I do like to talk about him. Never mind how sad it makes me feel."

"Do you think Mikey *could be* Firth?" I asked. Or is it a coincidence? I mean, Firth getting born again as Mikey? That's impossible, right?"

"I dinna scorn coincidence, lass?" Em said, "and nothing is impossible. Life's a grand mystery, aye. If we want to solve it, we start as you did a moment ago— ask questions. Don't think I mind, dearie, to answer your concerns. What a body who lives alone needs with a passion is stimilatin' conversation!"

Through the window I could see Mikey headed toward the back door, Malkin right behind him. Rain again mixed with streaks of morning sunlight.

"Know what?" Mikey asked as he entered the kitchen, the cat at his heels.

"What, Mikey?" I exchanged looks with Em.

"I saw a rabbit!" He laughed. "Brown and gray and white. With whiskers!"

I let out my breath. "That's *all?*"

The letdown feeling I had then confused me. I should've been relieved that Mikey hadn't had another flash from his so-called past life.

Admit it, I told myself, you're disappointed.

I was. I wanted to know *more*.

✤ fIVE ✤

"EM, I HAD THE strangest dream last night. Want to hear it?"

"Aye, I do. I love dreams, lass. All my life I've taken pleasure and comfort analyzing my dreams. Look on my old bookshelf in your room, you'll find a book or three on the subject. Tell me your dream, Christie, I'm all ears."

"I dreamed about a piper," I began, "at first I thought it was you because the person at the top of the hill wore a skirt. Then I realized it was a kilt, not a skirt."

Mikey sat at the kitchen table next to Em. While I talked, he crayoned colorful doodles on a page of his Doodle Pad.

Haltingly...as best I could remember...I described my dream to Em. I felt strange telling her, probably because I'd never told anyone a dream before. Even so, when I finished telling her about the piper, I hummed the tune he'd played.

Mikey glanced up at me, his eyes wide. "He wore the kilt?" he asked in an awed voice. "What colors, Christie?"

"I didn't get that close, Mikey."

"I recognize the tune," Em said.

"So what do you think? Do you think I dreamed the piper, or could he be real? Like some young guy who lives close by?"

"Canna think of any young man who pipes," she replied, "unless—"

"Unless—what, Em?"

"Nothing, just a stray, foolish thought. Doesna amount to an answer." She got up from the table to look out the window over the sink.

From my seat at the kitchen table I could see my own view of the backyard garden, past a row of pink, white, and lavender hollyhocks, to the foot of the rocky path up Lauder Hill.

"I heard him, though—" I said, "his music, loud and clear. He was *good*, Em. I mean, he played well. I'd never heard bagpipe music, at least, none that I remember."

I waited for her to say something. When she still didn't turn around or answer me, I began to feel embarrassed that I'd talked so much. Is she even interested? I wondered.

"I *did* like the pipe music he played, though," I said, maybe a little too loudly. Why wasn't Em paying attention anyway? Hadn't she said she *loved* dreams?

When she turned away from the window to face me again, and began to talk, I relaxed. She had been listening to me, after all.

"You're not the only one to see a piper, dearie. All sorts of locations, remote or populated, hill and dale, daylight or midnight. Not such a rare sight to see a phantom piper in Scotland."

"*Phantom* piper?"

"Or a livin', breathin' one, practicin' his heart out,"

she added. "Lass, as I mentioned before, Scotland's a misty, mystical land. Funny happenings here."

"Yeahhh," I rolled my eyes. Mikey giggled.

"Aye, t'is true," Em went on, "many a visitor to Scotland has told of hearin' or catchin' sight of a ghost piper. They swear they'd seen a swirl of tartan, heard a skirl of the pipes, and then stood enthralled to listen.

"They'd argue long and hard if questioned that it was a true sightin' and hearin'. Truth is, lots of reliable folks, both native Scots and outsiders swear to the Invisibles."

"Em, wait a second—phantom pipers? Ghosts? Invisibles?" You're not serious, are you?"

She brushed the air in front of her face as if to swat a fly. I squinted suspiciously. I couldn't see any fly, but I *could* see the sparkles of mischief in her blue eyes.

"Serious? Only when I have to be, lassie."

"Okay, but you're saying what I saw last night was an *Invisible?* That only *I* could see it? And—" I thought for a few seconds, "—at the same time, seeing a piper in the middle of the night happens a lot in Scotland?"

Em's lined face took on a gloomy expression.

"Aye, Scotland itself and the Borders in particular —a treasure trove of mystic tales. I could tell you stories to set your fair wavy hair into corkscrew wires." She nodded darkly.

"Tales of banshees and beasties, ghouls and ghosties and things that go bump in the night."

"Go ahead," I dared her.

"Ghosties to start with," she said in raspy low voice. "Not many castles or hotels or ruined abbeys canna boast at least one restless spirit in residence.

And don't they! Good for business, ghosts are. Tourists expect them, ken?"

"I don't know about other tourists," I said, "but I didn't expect *any* of this weirdness. Anyway, Em, what kinds of ghosts?"

"Here we've got all kinds," she assured me. "Tragic Green Ladies of olden times, wailin' and wanderin' the moors. Green's the favorite color, but Pink Ladies as well. Warriors on horseback. Entire armies have been seen, and singular knights without heads, lone pipers, troupes of dancers, and dinna forget, the Wee People.

"Again, lass, on Scottish soil, roamin' departed spirits are plentiful. Could come from all the gloomy, doomy, bloody history of centuries past."

I stared at her, caught between fascination and fear. I liked the way her voice sounded, like music, her words the lyrics of a song."

"But ghosts aren't real, Em—right? You said yourself they're only stories."

"Think so?" Em answered. "Take this one. It's often told, poor Mary o'Scots comes round to Borthwick Castle grounds where she'd come as a bride. Wanders 'round dressed in a page boy's guise, forlorn and tragic-faced. Who can blame her for lookin' disappointed-like. Not easy for the poor thing, spendin' her afterlife carryin' aboot her own head under her arm."

"Em, that's disgusting!" I couldn't help but giggle. "'Poor Mary' is right, but—back up for a second! I haven't figured out what a *past life* is yet, and now you're giving me *afterlife*? What's an *afterlife*?"

"Now I've done it," she said. "Yer mither will have my head when she hears what I've been telling you two."

"She won't hear," I promised. "Not from me."

The last thing I wanted now, I decided, was for Em to clam up. Never mind that some of what she'd said I didn't much like. She was my only source of information. "And Mikey won't tell her, will you, Mikey?" I put my finger to my lips. "Don't tell Mommy any ghost stories. Mommy doesn't like ghosts!"

His eyes got wider. "How come?"

I shrugged. "She doesn't believe in them, I guess. Come to think of it, I don't either."

At the kitchen sink, Em had her back to us. "I've got garden work to tend to," she said. "Best time for pullin' weeds is morning. Want to help, you two?"

"Sure, come on, Mikey and Malkin. Let's go out and help Em. Maybe later I'll take you for a walk, peanut, how's that?"

I'd thought if I helped Em in the garden she'd keep being talkative, continue with her stories, explain more about what she'd already said. I was wrong.

By the time she'd put on a pair of tall green rubber boots which she called "Wellies," found an extra pair for me, and still another "wee" set of boots for Mikey, her mind was fixed only on her garden chores. All she would say is how much she liked to be quiet in order to hear her garden grow.

I got what she meant, her polite way of telling me not to talk to her.

For a while I pretended interest in her veggies and herbs, but as I pulled weeds, I thought about my dream. After a while I had to break the silence.

Mikey sat with Malkin on the stone bench, far enough away from us so he couldn't hear. "Em, if so many other people have seen phantom pipers, I wonder—have you?"

Just by the sheepish expression on her face when she looked over at me, I felt sure she'd tell me she had. Wrong again.

"Not me, Christie. Never so fortunate." She sighed. "Some day—not now—I'll tell you about Lauder pipers. All gone but ne'er forgotten."

"I'd like to hear," I said and meant it.

For another half hour Mikey and I hung around the garden with Em. As soon as I could decently do it, I found a way for us to go off on our own. I asked about the old bicycles she'd mentioned the night before.

Em pointed me to the shed at the back of her walled yard.

The wooden door hung crooked on its hinges. When I pulled back the old door, it made a loud creaking sound, perfect background noise for Em's ghost stories, I decided.

Since Mikey hadn't learned to ride a two-wheeler yet, I chose the best of the two old bicycles—best because it had a wide, sturdy wire basket attached to the front handlebars. The basket would make the perfect passenger seat for Mikey.

It took only a few minutes to wipe away most of the grime and cobwebs with an old rag I found in the shed. Afterwards, I wheeled the clumsy, rusty contraption to the front of the castle. With a few practice rides, I knew I could handle it well enough, even with the added weight of Mikey in the basket.

Except—where would we go? I wondered.

All the while I'd worked to get ready for a ride to check out the neighborhood—if there was a neighborhood—I'd had the strongest urge to check out Lauder Hill instead. No matter how I tried to put it out of my mind, I couldn't forget my dream.

"Come on, peanut," I said, "we'll go for a ride later. Let's climb the hill now, okay?"

In her shiny green hat, slicker, and boots, Em blended with the garden. I finally spotted her halfway between what she'd called her "bonny wee pea-patch" and a bed of purple petunias. I let her know where we were headed.

"For today," she said, "don't stray far. Stay in sight of Castle Lauder. 'T would be hard to get lost, but for now, I wouldna want to go back on my word to your Mum." She gave me a guilty look. "Not any more than I've already done, that is."

"You haven't, Em," I assured her. "I'm the one who asked so many questions, remember?"

Em brushed her gray hair back from her face. She glanced up at Mikey, studied his face for a moment, then looked down at her own muddy hands. *"Remember?"* She smiled sadly, "now isna that a word and a ha'?"

She sounded so depressed, I didn't know what to say, so I turned and walked away without saying anything.

Mikey didn't appear to mind my sudden change of plan. He tagged along with me, sweet and cooperative, the little brother I knew best. For once since we'd arrived at Castle Lauder, the gray cat wasn't around.

As we climbed up the narrow, rock-strewn path, I purposely walked behind and a bit to one side of Mikey. The last thing I wanted to happen was for him to catch sight of the creepy leafless tree over to the left of us. I didn't want him to freak out as he had yesterday.

On purpose, too, I'd kept a slow pace—not sure if

Mikey should be climbing at all, only a day after an asthma attack. He looked and sounded fine so far, but—

Halfway up the winding path, I stopped. "Like this?" I asked. "Look at the castle, Mikey. Doesn't it look smaller?"

My brother pointed past me. "Christie, I don't like that tree. It's ugly and twisty and—*yucky!* I *hate* that tree!"

I knelt down and put my arm around him. "Don't look at it then," I said. "Pretend it's invisible. Hey, peanut, I don't see any old tree, do you? No sir, no tree on this hill!"

He whimpered. "I see it, Christie."

"Yeah," I admitted, hugging him close. "I see it, too. And you're right, sweetie, it is a yucky tree. Don't look at it anymore."

The sun shone on the bramble bushes, green leaves and bright yellow blossoms on either side of the narrow stone path. Just ahead I caught sight of a large, flat rock. The rock glinted silver in the sunlight. "Come on, peanut, let's take a break. Sit with me awhile."

I wished now I hadn't encouraged Em to talk about dream pipers or headless knights or—ghosts! If he had nightmares it would be my fault. I'd probably have a few nightmares myself, I thought.

Beside me, Mikey gave the rock several taps.

"I 'member this stone, Christie," he said. "When I was bigger I sat here. Lots of times I sat here."

"Mikey!" How could he remember a rock? A castle, maybe, but not a rock? A single stone?

"You're making that up, aren't you? You're being silly, right? You want me to pretend? Okay, Mikey, I believe you. When you were big, this rock was your special place. You sat on it all the time, you and—"

I clamped one hand over my mouth before I said the name—Calinda!

What's the matter with me? The sun was out, it was broad daylight, and I couldn't think of any good reason why I should be so scared. I was, though. I looked at my brother, so small and helpless and innocent-looking. With all my heart, I wanted to grab him up and run with him down the rocky path, past the castle, to the lane, to the road—away from here.

The fear—it had come out of nowhere! I wrapped my arms around my middle and squeezed until the feeling ebbed away.

"Christie?" Mikey patted my arm. "You crying?"

"No, no, just the wind, honey. My eyes are watering from the breeze, that's all. Don't look so worried."

"Em says ghosts—"

"Mikey, don't worry about ghosts, either!" I fought to keep calm. "Em was only telling us stories. You know about stories. Some I read you from a book at bedtime. Sometimes, I put the book away and make up a story from my head? Like that, Mikey—that's what Em did."

I hugged him. "Don't be scared, peanut, there's no such thing as ghosts."

He looked at me with the strangest expression as I babbled on. "Christie?"

"What?"

"When I'm a ghost, I see me hanging from the yucky tree. 'Cept the tree isn't yucky—it's *good* n'green. Yup, it's a good tree."

"Mikey, don't..."

"I sit on this rock. I cry."

"Mikey—"

"Not all the time," he whispered. "Sometimes I go away to the big light. I fly away from the tree and the stones."

"You're making this up."

"I do, Christie. I fly in the sky to the big light. I like it, it's nice."

"Stop it!" He scared me because—"Mikey, people—especially little peanuts like you—can't fly."

But he didn't giggle as I hoped he would. "I do. I can! Sometimes.

"Christie, don't be mad. Are you mad?"

"No, 'course not. Come on," I said in the sweetest, calmest voice I could manage. "Let's go back down. It's too windy up here. Right now I could use a cup of tea."

He scrambled off the rock and gave me his hand to hold.

I took his hand, warmed it with mine for a minute, then dropped it. "You first, peanut," I said, "go on, I'm right behind you."

All the way down the hill I fought back the tears. Real tears, hot enough to burn the back of my eyelids. I hadn't cried much since my father died and I knew if I gave in and let the tears flow, I'd never get them to stop.

By the time I reached the castle, I felt shaky but I had myself under control. Beside the back entry-way door, Malkin waited for Mikey.

In the kitchen, Em sat alone at the table.

"Cuppa tea?" she asked when we walked in. "A wee bit to eat?"

"Yes," I told her, "and after that, a nap. Maybe Mikey will take one, too."

More than a nap, what I really wanted was some time alone in the tower room. If I did give in to tears again, at least I could do it without anyone else around.

"Aye," Em said, "tea and hot scones. Good for what ails ye."

I wished it were true.

✦ SIX ✦

"HERE, PEANUT, CURL UP on the couch with Malkin," I said. "Sleep for a bit, I will too. When we get up we'll go for a bike ride—promise."

By the time I left the parlor Mikey's eyelids were already three-quarters closed. Nestled against his chest, only his gray head visible, Malkin purred a lullaby.

I returned to the kitchen. "If Mikey wakes up before I do, call me," I told Em. She nodded that she would, but still I lingered in the doorway. It took several seconds longer to build up my nerve.

"Please," I said, "tell me about that tree on the back slope. It couldn't be the hanging tree, could it? The one—"

"Aye, it could and it is," she said. "Over fifty years that tree has stood, never to bloom again. Inexplicable, that tortured, twisted tree. A constant grim reminder of Firth."

"It *is* creepy, Em."

"Aye, t'is creepy and sad. Once the tree was sturdy and vital, a joy to behold, with healthy leaves and fragrant wee blossoms.

"Bees loved it," she said, "birds nested in it, and

Firth and I climbed its welcoming branches. Often as not, it sheltered us during a sudden downpour. The tree was a family friend, you might say—no more."

As she spoke, Em gazed into space. Her blue eyes held dark shadows of painful memory and the muscles of her face sagged.

"I'm sorry," I said, "but I had to know because the tree bothers Mikey a lot, too.

"Another thing, when we climbed the hill today, Mikey said he remembered a big rock at the side of the path. I don't think he could remember a rock, do you?"

She jolted as if she'd been asleep. "What, lass? I didn't quite catch what you said."

"Not important. Are you…all right?"

She nodded. "I'm right as the rain, Christie. Run up now, and rest your bonny head. Private time—sweet solitude—is what a lass your age needs. Take it while ye can."

Private time! Solitude! She understood!

"Thanks," I said and flashed her a grateful smile over my shoulder before I hurried up the stone stairway to the tower room. I hadn't intended to like Emma Lauder, but it was hard not to.

Rather than waste all my private time on a nap, I got out my journal and made a list of the strange things Mikey had said.

1. *When he was "bigger" (bigger than Daddy!)*
2. *His name was FIRTH (not "first")*
3. *As Firth, he got hanged*
4. *He lived here in Castle Lauder*
5. *He knew to turn right to get to Castle Lauder*

6. *He said "Hi" to Em as if he knew her*
7. *Same with the cat*
8. *Said he remembered Em's "good hair"*
9. *Says "didna" for "didn't," and "Ed-in-bur-rah," the same way Em pronounces the words*
10. *Remembers the "hanging tree" on the hill*
11. *Remembers a large flat stone on the hill???*
Fact: FIRTH LAUDER IS THE NAME OF EM'S DEAD BROTHER, HANGED FROM THE TREE ON THE HILL OVER FIFTY YEARS AGO!

Propped up by bed pillows, I studied my list, certain I'd forgotten all kinds of important clues, and facts to remember. At last, I turned to a new page in my journal.

Except I didn't begin writing immediately. I couldn't help but wonder if I should bother. Not only could I be making a great big deal about nothing, but I could make trouble for myself—for Mikey, and Em, too. Mom wouldn't be at all happy if she knew I'd pumped Em for information. Still, why shouldn't I try to find out? What else was there to do here at Castle Lauder? Besides, I couldn't help but be curious. For my next list I would write down my questions.

1. *How did Mikey know?*
2. *"Reincarnation"—What is it? How does it work? Is it possible? Past life?*
3. *GHOSTS?*
4. *The Piper in my dream?*
5. *FAIRIES—wee people—fairyfolk?*

6. *DEATH—(most important). Why? How does it work?*
7. *Calinda Douglas? (Ask Em!)*
8. *Does Lauder have a library? Look up the Lauder family and Malcolm family.*
9. *How could I remember the Piper's music? (Em says the tune I hummed this morning sounded like a song she knows.)*

I'd run out of space on the page, but I turned to the next page, unsatisfied with what I'd written so far. Before I'd begun the lists, I'd been sure the clues and questions I had been carrying around in my mind since our arrival would pour out onto the pages. I could see for myself how little I knew about anything. I had so many questions and so few answers. I wanted—more!

Finally, I put away my pen and journal and snuggled in among the pillows. I spotted a plaid blanket folded at the bottom of the bed. Good old Em, she thought of everything.

Before I allowed myself to sink into sleep, I made a decision. To keep from forgetting or losing important clues or questions, from now on I wouldn't leave this room without my mini-cassette recorder. The little recorder, identical to the one Mom carried in her briefcase, had been a Christmas gift. I hadn't used it much, but now I was glad I'd remembered to pack it.

From this moment on, I decided, I would keep the tiny recorder with me. This way, whenever Mikey—or anyone—said something important, I'd have it on tape.

When I did sleep, I slept deeply, but not for long. I sat up in bed with a start, glanced at my watch, and was shocked to find that only twenty minutes had passed. Strange, though, I felt full of energy.

I no longer felt anxious and scared. Whatever happened now, I thought, I'd be ready. If I kept alert, soon enough I would discover the answers I needed—answers to make sense of all the weirdness.

With the mini-recorder in my pocket I went downstairs.

Not only did I find Mikey awake when I entered the parlor, he proudly held up a sheet of paper covered all over with criss-crossed crayoned lines. On the floor beside him were other papers colored nearly the same, in straight lines: red, green, black, blue.

"Like 'em, Christie?" he asked proudly. "This one's for you. It's *the kilt!*"

"Oh," I said, puzzled. Then, to keep him happy, I folded the paper carefully and slipped it into my back pocket. 'I'll keep it forever. Hey, come on, little brother, let's go riding!"

Before I left the castle, I found Em to let her know we'd be outside. She smiled, pointed to a floppy pillow on the kitchen bench and told me to line the bicycle basket with it.

"Less of a bumpy ride for the lad," she added. I left her to her cooking of a dish which definitely smelled fishy. I decided not to ask what it was, although most fish and seafood I did like.

I walked the heavy bike to the front of the castle, put Mikey in the basket and climbed on. After a few minutes of severe front-wheel wobble, I got us going smoothly. I couldn't see Mikey's expression, but from the noises he made, I knew he loved it.

"Want me to go faster, squirt? Let's pretend I'm a racing car driver...here I go, Mikey. Hold on!"

His squeal of excitement made me feel good. At least I could give him a little fun once in a while, I thought.

And for what my leg muscles told me was a long time, I wheeled him around the curving driveway, up and down the walled lane and back again—faster and faster. By this time, Mikey was really into it, yelling and laughing like a little fiend.

That's how Mom found us, and as she inched the rental car alongside us, she gave me a big smile and a thumbs up sign.

"Oh, Christie," she said, when she got out of the car, "it does my heart good to find you two having so much fun here. I hoped you'd get to like it, and now you have, and—great!—I can say I *did* make the right decision to stay at Castle Lauder!"

She surprised me. Had she actually worried that she hadn't? Did it really matter to her if I liked it here with Em? For a minute I let myself look at her—really look at her face, her eyes, her hair. Except for her height—I'm two inches taller already—I would look like her when I finished growing up. In that minute, I loved her again. Loved her hard, with all my might.

"We're winning—Indy 500—gotta go!" I called as I pedaled furiously away. "See ya, Mom."

When I looked back over my shoulder, I spotted her standing with her work paraphernalia piled at her feet, her camera bag, portfolio, notebooks, and Daddy's briefcase. She just stood as if she were lost in her own thoughts. She'd sounded cheerful when she'd spoken a moment ago. But right now the way she stood, her head bent, shoulders slumped, she looked sad to me.

As I pedaled off in the other direction, I couldn't

help but feel sorry for her. Athough she didn't mention it much, I knew she had to be missing my father, too.

I'd tensed up and Mikey noticed. He craned his neck around, gave me one long look, then smiled uncertainly.

Immediately, I slowed my speed and braked the bicycle to a full stop. "Let's go back," I said. "I mean, let's make a quick pit stop. We'll help Mommy bring in her stuff, okay?"

"'Kay," he said. "Good ride, Christie."

I ruffled his hair. "Yeah," I agreed.

Mom accepted our help, and it was thanks enough that her face and eyes brightened up again.

"Might as well stay in now," I told Mikey. "I bet Malkin misses you."

"I miss Malkin, too," he said. "Em, too."

Lucky kid, I thought, he has Malkin, me, Mom, and Em to miss him, care about him. All at once I felt sad and lonesome. Maybe, I thought gloomily, my mother had passed along her blue mood to me.

As we passed the part of the back garden where Em's herbs were, I stopped walking and looked long and hard at all the bright flowers, plump vegetables, and glowing greenery all around us. I took a deep breath, then another one, and lifted my chin. For Mikey's sake, I would try to stay in a decent mood.

"We'll do another Indy tomorrow, pal," I promised.

After supper, later in the evening, Em asked aloud, "I've been thinkin'. Truth is, I've been longin' for this chance. Who'd like to beat me at a swift game of cards? Christie, how about you? Think you can kick my breeks at Gin Rummy? It's been years 'tween games for this natural-born sharp!"

"Sounds good to me," I answered. Actually, it did.

Before Em and I could get to our card game, though, she had the dishes to wash up, and I had Mikey to wash up and put to bed. No chance of Mom taking over, since, as she had declared over supper: "I have homework, tons of it! So much more to learn about tartans and the tartan trade than I ever thought possible!"

Mom ate quickly. She didn't linger long over coffee, either. I could tell she was anxious to get off by herself, to pore over the pamphlets and books she'd brought home. More than likely, she'd spend the evening reading, making notes and sketching.

Easy, I warned myself. Anyway, why should I get mad at her for not paying attention. What else is new?

"Later, after I get it all straight in my own mind," Mom had said over her shoulder as she left the kitchen, "I'll tell you about my day. It's fascinating, Christie!"

I forced myself to smile back at her. "Okay, Mom—great!"

Later, though, as I sat at the small table before a cozy fire, I felt better. I shuffled the deck of worn-thin playing cards.

Em seated herself opposite me. "Ye get first deal, lass."

But first deal didn't help. We played three games and each time Em kicked my britches, or *breeks*—her word—all three times. Was she ever proud of herself! She gloated. She blew on her hands, then rubbed them together with satisfaction.

"Och, dearie, that felt good. Havna' lost my auld touch, after a'."

She made me laugh as she carried on like a kid over her big wins. "Ah, but next time, Em," I warned, "*next* time, just you wait!"

Except my gladness over seeing her have fun turned bittersweet when it hit me who she reminded me of—my father!

Either way, win or lose, Daddy would turn into a raving maniac. If he'd lost the game—any game—he'd rant that I'd cheated. If he won, he'd rave on and on about how great he was, how no one could beat him.

Yeah, sure, I thought, no one except death.

While Em banked the fire for the night, I fitted the cards back into their cardboard case. After that I carried our teacups into the kitchen, and washed and rinsed them before she joined me.

Malkin crouched before his food on the floor. His faintly striped gray tail twitched fair warning not to bother him while he ate his late supper. "Don't worry, cat," I said aloud.

"Thank ye, lass," Em said. "Now it's bed for me. Your mither's been up the stairs for—how long?" She glanced at the round clock above the long, dish-and-jar-cluttered sideboard.

"Midnight!" she exclaimed. "I'm awa' wi' the fairies, keeping you up so late!"

"No problem, Em," I told her. "It was fun. We'll do it again, won't we?"

"Aye, dear. Now go up before ye mither has me head twice."

Her saying that reminded me. "Em, wait, guess what I did? You said to write down my questions for Dr. Dalvercroft. I did write them, this afternoon, but a couple of answers, you'd have, so—"

"Lass—"

"Please, Em, just one?"

She sighed. "Aye, one."

"You told me your brother got hanged on a June night. What night exactly? I mean, what was the date? I figure if I have to look up the legend in the library, I'll need—"

"June eighteen, nineteen hundred and—"

"You're kidding!"

Em gave me a fierce look. "Kidding, lass? *Nae, nae,* I wouldn't kid."

I knew I'd said it wrong, but I couldn't believe it.

"Em," I whispered, barely able to get the words out. "June eighteenth is Mikey's birthday! Is that incredible or what?"

She pulled out a chair from the table and sat down on it heavily. Em appeared to be as stunned as I felt.

With both gnarled hands pressed against her heart, she stared back at me. For the first time since I'd met her she had the look of a feeble old woman.

"I wouldna let myself hope," she said in a cracked voice. "As I promised your mither, I tried to put my deepest hopes on the back burner. Not that the idea of rebirth is strange to me. A gardener such as meself knows well about nature's returns. The Good Book says it like this, 'For everything there's a season...a time to sow, a time to reap...a time to live, a time to die'—but, och, Christie, you brother—*mine?* Firth come back again?"

Em wasn't crying. Not yet, but her voice cracked and quavered with every word. And with every word, I expected her to lower her head to her arms and bawl her heart out.

Any second now I expected myself to do the same.

"Could it be true, Em?" I whispered. "Or just another...coincidence?"

I didn't believe that. She didn't either, I could tell.

"Lord ha' mercy, if t'is true, my dear brother left this earth through one door," she whispered. "Then, through the same door, fifty-some years later, enters your precious brother. I dinna ken, yet I do hope now."

"A *door?* Is that how death works, Em? People die and go through a door?"

"In a manner of speaking, aye," she said, her voice slightly stronger. "Go t'bed, lass. Come morning, I'll be phoning up Ian!"

✤ seven ✤

OUTSIDE MY TOWER-ROOM window the wind went wild.

I tossed and turned. No matter what I tried, sleep wouldn't come to my rescue. If Em thought midnight a late bedtime, I wondered what she'd think if she could see me now, stark, wide-eyed, at three in the morning.

If only I could've switched off my mind. Questions about Daddy, questions about death, the same ones I'd asked myself for months, wouldn't stop. Repeated over and over, like a ruined tape, the one-word question appeared and sounded in my mind: *Why?*

Why, Daddy? Why did you leave me when I still need you so much? Why?

Except for my brother, my father had been my best friend. All my life he'd been the only one I could really count on to understand me and take my side. Mom always said Daddy and I were a lot alike—as she put it, "peas from the same pod."

Under the covers, as I listened to the whine and wail of the wind outside, I remembered how both my parents used to tease me. They'd called me a "regular little homebody."

During the first years when Mom went back to work, and Daddy took a second job to help pay Mikey's medical bills, I hadn't minded too much. I was younger then. I guess it made me feel important and proud of myself for being part of what we had called our "family management team."

I'd never protested later either, even after family finances got better, and we moved to the new house. If I had asked for more time to myself, if I had refused to be Mikey's second mother and live-in babysitter, would I have gotten my way?

Even if I'd opened my mouth and told them—

No, I thought. What good would it have done? They'd needed to believe I was perfectly happy, a great daughter, a cheerful, unselfish, always loving sister. And they'd liked to believe I had a choice!

Even if I'd wanted friends and a social life—anyway, too late now. No one except my family knew I existed. Besides, I would've worried too much about Mikey. How could I trust any other person—some stranger!—to take care of him? To love him?

Daddy, why did you die? Why did you? What makes people be alive one day, and dead the next? Why is anyone born if all that ends up happening is death? Why...bother?

Flat on my back in bed, arms straight at my sides, I cried without making a sound. The wail and screech of the wind made enough noise, a perfect match for what I felt inside: restless, wild, so lonely and sad and mad, I couldn't stand it anymore.

Tears slid from the corners of my eyes directly into my hair. *Oh, Daddy—help! Tell me what to do!*

Exhausted, I closed my eyes. All I could do was

wait for morning to come. It would be hours yet until dawn but—

Then—I couldn't figure out how it happened—I found myself outdoors in the dark at the foot of Lauder Hill!

Am I dreaming?

Why, then, I wondered, did I still feel wide awake, able to think...to feel the chill air and wind against my skin?

My body felt different, though, lighter somehow, and as I began the climb up the stony path, I didn't hesitate or stumble in the dark. As I climbed upward I began to imagine myself as a balloon, light, free, able to lift off the ground and float, rather than use my legs and feet.

I could see nothing except the thick green darkness and drifts of white mist. The wind sounded to me like music. As I moved faster and faster up the hill, I knew it was music.

Sad music...the sound more like a person wailing and crying than actual music.

As I thought that, hot tears filled my eyes. *I* felt the fiercest urge to wail and sob.

And, right then, with my eyes blinded by hot tears, I had the strongest sense that someone waited for me at the top of the hill. Someone who made me feel sad and glad at the same time. Someone I couldn't wait to see again...the Piper!

Down to me, down through the thin cobwebs of mist, past the craggy outcrops of silvery granite, flowed the music of the pipes.

Part of me doubted it could really be happening, but another part of me knew that I would see him. I would stand beside him, and, up close, hear his music.

Just as I thought that, the music stopped. After a pause, I heard his voice. I stood still and listened as he sang.

> And fare thee weel, my only love,
> ...and fare thee weel a while—
> And I weel come again, my love,
> though it were ten-thousand mile...

I struggled to move, to climb the rest of the way up the hill. *Why couldn't I move?*

He sang the words as if he meant them, as if he felt them. I thought of my first sight of the Piper and how I'd described him to Em—Confusing, though. If I could think of Em, and remember what I'd said to her, how could this be a dream?

I *felt* awake—wide, wide awake. So why couldn't I move my feet? They seemed to be stuck fast in something thick and white and lumpy like...porridge.

Fare thee weel, he'd sung. Had he gone? No, I could hear the pipes again. To me, the pipe music sounded like a violin, trumpet, and accordian all mixed together.

Most important, though, I recognized the song as the same one I'd remembered and hummed for Em.

My chest hurt as I tried to force my body upward on the dark, narrow path. Heavy as lead, useless, my arms hung at my sides. My feet, my legs were stones; they wouldn't budge an inch.

"Stay there," I yelled. "Wait for me!"

One glimpse, I thought, that's all I ask. If only I could see him, just to know he's real, know he's more than a dream.

In answer to my silent wish, when I looked up again, I could see through the thin veils of mist.

Him. Solid. Real. Not a dream.

Not daring to breathe, I stared up at him. He gazed back at me.

The Piper took a step forward. He bent his head toward me and as we looked at each other, I...*I knew I knew him!*

I didn't know why or how I knew him, but I did. The Piper wasn't a stranger to me, even if I couldn't imagine how this could be true.

In his kilt, heavy sweater, with the pipes in his arms, he stood solid, flesh-and-blood real. A few years older than me, maybe. He took a step forward, bent closer. I saw his mouth move. His lips formed a word.

I strained toward him, unable to hear what he said.

At my back I felt a strong pull. As helpless as a straight pin drawn to a magnet, I couldn't resist the force that pulled me backwards down the path.

Down...down...until I found myself back where I'd started, at the foot of Lauder Hill.

As I shivered in the chilly darkness, bewildered and frustrated, into my mind came Em's words, "Look deeply, lass, see what others canna see."

I wanted to believe that I had seen him, that it hadn't been a dream or what my mother would call "wishful thinking."

I listened hard but all I heard, for sure, was the low, mournful whine of the wind.

My skin felt wet...icy cold.

Why...why did you leave me? Why did you have to go?

Now I had another question. Who was this piper?

And why had he called to me, sung to me? What had he been trying to tell me?

Why had he looked so familiar? In all my life I'd never met anyone who looked like him.

A dream...only a dream. It had to be, because the next thing I knew I sat up in bed shivering.

Gray early morning light filled the round room. Through the wide-open back window I could feel the cold damp breeze. No wonder my skin felt so clammy, icy cold.

I sat there. Through the open window, past the threads of mist, I studied the rock-solid outline of Lauder Hill.

I looked at the hill out there and knew the answer, even if I didn't want it to be true.

In the middle of the night, I'd finally fallen asleep. I had dreamed. That's all it was, I thought, just another silly piper dream, and—

I heard a knock on the door. "Come in," I croaked.

"Oh, good, sweetie, you're up."

I slid back down against the pillows. "Not really, Mom."

"But I need you to get up, Christie," she said, then made a face. "This room is absolutely frigid. Christie, it may be summer, but I don't think keeping your window wide open all night to the wind—or, maybe, *bats*—is a very good idea.

"And, look at you, you're shaking. Hey, the last thing I need today is for you to get sick. I've got to leave here in the next few minutes if I intend to get anything accomplished."

Hardly ever, and, probably, never, have I lied to my

mother as I lied right then. "I *am* sick, Mom. Already."
I forced a cough, and without having to try hard,
another shiver. "Sorry, but my throat is killing me! I
can barely swallow."

Mom hurried across the room to close the window,
then returned to my bedside. She wrinkled up her brow
as she stared down at me. "Put on your robe and slippers, come downstairs, have some juice and toast, and
I'll go find the Tylenol."

"Mom, I—"

She tried to hide it, but I saw the brief flash of
annoyance in her eyes. If I'd been able to read her
mind, I guessed her thoughts went something like,
*How can you do this to me? I counted on you. Now,
thanks to you, Christie, I'll have to change my plans!
How dare you get sick!*

Or—maybe not. Her hand on my forehead and her
voice when she leaned over me was soft and sympa-
thetic. "Mmm, honey, you don't seem to have any fever.
Anyway, don't worry about a thing, lie back, relax. I'll
bring you the tea, toast and Tylenol."

Now I really did feel terrible. "What about your
plans?" I mumbled, "I can get up, I don't think
it's...serious."

"No," my mother said, smiling at me. "You stay in
bed, sweetie. I'll leave anyway—have Em keep a sharp
eye out for you two. I like her, don't you?"

"Don't know her yet," I said, closing my eyes.

"Christie!"

My eyelids popped open. "What?"

"What's your new robe doing on the floor. And
your new white slippers, all wet and muddy, with

bits of—where were you to get these so dirty?"

"Nowhere."

She sounded furious. "Christie, were you outside last night roaming the grounds in your night clothes? No wonder you're sick this morning? Look at this, stickyburrs and pieces of heather all over your slippers and the hem of your robe!"

Even if I'd been able to think of an answer, I wouldn't have been able to get the words out of my mouth.

Last night, when I'd climbed into bed, the robe and slippers were perfectly fine, practically new...clean. Which *had* to prove I'd been outdoors at some time during the night.

Proof that my dream had *not* been a dream, *not* my imagination. It had happened. I'd actually climbed Lauder Hill and met the Piper.

The music of the pipes, his voice, the song—real!

I peeked at my mother through half-closed eyes. She still hovered over me. I could tell she expected an answer.

"Maybe I walked in my sleep?"

I watched her shake her head, then walk away toward the door. "Go back to sleep, Christie," she told me before she left the room. "Could be you need a day off from the real world."

"Thanks," I answered. When the door closed behind her, I opened my eyes wide and stared up at the ceiling. *Real world?* I wondered.

✤ eight ✤

EM STOOD BESIDE THE bed, her face solemn. "T'is my fault, keepin' you up all hours. Your mither told me you wandered out in the damp during the wee hours and now you're sick. You did that, lass? Why?"

"Em!" I sat up in bed. How could I not tell her? I had to tell someone. "I heard the pipes again. I don't remembering doing it, but I must've put on my robe and slippers before I climbed the hill.

"See?" I pointed to the soiled nightclothes. "I'm sure of it. Before I got into bed last night, they were clean and dry.

"You climbed the hill in the dark?" Em clucked. "You might've fallen, dearie."

"I can't explain. It's weird, but, Em, I heard him piping and he *sang*. I saw his face!

"Right now I can't remember exactly what he looked like, but what's really weird is he seemed familiar—someone I've met before." I thought for a second. "Maybe he just looks like someone I've seen in a magazine or a movie or—"

"Is there a piper around here? A young guy who lives in the...the neighborhood? Remember the first time I told you I saw him? I thought it was a dream, but now, I don't think so. How could I get my bathrobe all messed up in a dream?

"Em, he looked right at me. He said—"

"Och, lass," Em asked breathlessly, "what did he say?"

"That's just it, I don't know. I couldn't hear him then because I got pulled down the hill."

"Pulled?"

"I know, that sounds weird, too, but that's how it felt to me, which is why I figured it had to be a dream." I flopped back against the pillows. "Still, he looked so real...solid...nothing wispy or misty about him. Em, who *is* he?"

"You say he sang?"

"He did and, wait, I remember a little. He sang 'Fare thee well, my only love...' And then at the end the words went something like '...and I will come again...though it's ten thousand miles'—like that."

Em's eyes widened. "Christie, you've never heard that song before?"

I shook my head. "I'm pretty sure I haven't."

We were both quiet for a long moment. Em drew herself up, squared her shoulders, and when she broke the silence, changed the subject.

"Yer mither's off to her business and yer brother's down the hall in his room, sketchin' more grand, crayon designs, chattin' it up good with the Gray One. Not to worry, Christie, bairn and beastie are fine!"

"So my mother did take off? I knew she would."

"Aye, I urged her to go about her business. All dressed up and determined, she was. I told her if t'is only a head cold ye have, I'd be a capable-enough nurse." Her rosy skin made her blue eyes bluer, I noticed.

Not that I had any serious doubts about Em Lauder, but how long had we known her? Obviously my mother hadn't worried about leaving us in the care of a woman she barely knew. Still, I clamped my mouth shut and kept my opinion of Mom to myself. I couldn't deny it though. As usual, her lack of interest and attention bothered me, but especially today.

Even if I'd pretended not to feel well, she thought I didn't, and she'd still taken off, which really told me where I stood with her.

"Dearie, I phoned Ian—Dr. Dalvercroft—this morning," Em said. "The doctor I called for Mikey, ken? He's in Edinburgh for a bit, but when he returns, he'll come to visit.

"He holds a chair at the university. He'll be a good one for us to talk with about Mikey and, if you like, your own experience last night."

"He holds a *chair?* Why?" I stared at her. "What kind of chair? Is that a *job?*"

Em chuckled. "A distinguished position! I should tell ye, Christie. My friend, Ian, is brilliant. He holds the Parapsychology Chair at Edinburgh University. Another way of saying he's laird of his field of research!

"Parapsychology? What's that?"

"Ye'll ask him, dearie, but how I understand it, *para* means beyond. His field of inquiry would be *beyond* psychology."

"Psychology? But I want to know about reincarnation."

"He's done studies and research and can make logic 'round all the mysticals and magicals. Fascinatin' man, he is, and kindly." Em headed for the door.

"Ian's got a phone-answering contraption hooked

up. More than a wee intimidatin' to me. Not enough to keep me from leavin' a properly intimidatin' message back to him. I told his machine, 'Urgent mystic matters. Come soon for tea and cookies.'"

I laughed.

Not that I felt less confused, but at least now I could hope that Em's doctor friend would help me make sense of everything that had happened since we'd come to Scotland.

"Scoot down 'neath the covers and go back to sleep." She peered across the room at me. "Ye look more sleepy than sick, lass, but if it's a cold you caught, sleep will help chase it back where it came from. My hot barley soup will help, too, as well as a bedside visit with your brother. I'll bring both to ye in a short while."

"Thanks, Em." I'd never expected to like her, and, definitely, I hadn't wanted to get close to her. But this morning I did feel she could be the only person in the entire world who cared about me. Even Mikey seemed to be perfectly happy doing his own thing. Quite a few times now he'd made it clear to me that he preferred Em's or the cat's company to mine.

At the door Em stopped and looked at me over her shoulder. I could tell she wanted to say something, but she left without another word.

All morning long I stayed in bed. Once, though, I got up to inspect the books, which Em told me had been her favorites as a girl. I discovered a book about dreams and a slim volume of Robert Burns's poems and songs. I carried both books back to bed with me.

Over and over again, I read "My Love Is Like a Red, Red Rose." I closed my eyes tightly a few times and tried to recall the Piper's face, but I couldn't quite do it.

It did feel good, though, not to have to be responsible for a single soul except myself.

Em brought me soup and biscuits on a tray. Delicious soup, too, thick with all kinds of veggies from her garden.

By late afternoon, I felt restless and considered going down the stairs to join Mom, Mikey, and Em for tea. I decided against it. The truth was I didn't feel much like talking, especially not to my mother. She'd act and talk as if she'd done nothing wrong. To her, probably, she hadn't. She wouldn't understand for a second how she'd hurt me.

Right then I made up my mind to keep on playing sick. I'd stay in bed tomorrow and the next day, too, if I felt like it. Would Mom care? Eventually, would she start to worry about me?

Wait and see, I thought.

But my mother simply decided that since I was "under the weather," she'd take Mikey with her on her business trips around the countryside. Mikey loved it. When they returned the next afternoon, he had to tell me in detail everything he'd seen and done.

I listened to his tales of visits to museums and archives, old-time weavers' establishments, and other historic sites. Although I listened and tried to share his excitement, I began to feel sad and totally left out. The truth was, I was sick of playing sick.

The following morning I woke early, got dressed, and went down to the kitchen before Mom and Mikey were awake.

Em looked up and grinned. "Good to see ye among the livin', lass."

"Thanks," I said. "I feel fine."

I couldn't be sure, but the brief, sharp-eyed glance she sent my way, gave me the idea that she'd known all along that I'd been play-acting.

After breakfast Mom went off alone. For a while I watched Em work in her garden. She glanced up at me once, asked me if I'd like to 'yank weeds.' What could I say? After the first few minutes, though, I began to get into it. Weed-yanking helped me to put my thoughts and questions in order, and, soon, into words.

While Mikey concentrated on a new crayon and pencil drawing, at the opposite end of the garden, I got Em to tell me more about her dead brother.

"Just like Wee Mikey, Firth dearly loved to sketch and paint. Early on, he announced that he would travel to France and Italy to become a painter. As he put it, 'I'll paint my fool head off until I'm rich, fat, and famous.'"

Em smiled sadly. "Instead Firth went all practical and serious on us. He traveled only to Edinburgh to become an architect. Good at it, too. When my brother got...when he died, young man though he was, he'd already had a few notable successes. We were proud of him. Och, I know *I* was!"

I also got her to talk about Calinda Douglas. It was clear by her voice that Calinda's sad end still pained her a lot.

"Firth was daft 'bout her," Em explained. "He loved her with a' that was in him. A 'grand passion,' ye could call it. Calinda had charm, beauty and grace, and alertness of mind. A smart pair, they made, and both so talented! She liked to write and make up stories. Firth and Calinda told me they planned, one day, to collaborate on a book for children. She'd do the writin', he'd do the pictures, and they both agreed the subject would be the Wee People, and this magical Border Land.

"How anyone could be so cruel as to murder a dear lass as Calinda, I canna understand."

"Em," I asked, "what about the Lauder piper? You said you'd tell me about him."

"I'm glad to tell ye," Em said quietly. "In olden times, each clan had its own bard to keep track of important family events. A piper, as well, to play at mealtimes, celebrations, all manner of special occasions.

"A good piper puts to melody a clan's unique spirit. Music is a pattern, lass. Each clan has its own, a special pattern—pauses, tones and overtones, colors and codes.

"The songs reflect a' that. Lauder has its own songs and plaid, but Lauders belong to a *sept*, not a clan—the clan is Maitland. The sept Lauder is attached to the Maitland clan, ken?"

I nodded. "I think so. A *sept* would be like a branch of the main family. Go on."

"Uncle Peter, our father's brother, was a Lauder piper. He had the high talent for the pipes. He even went to study at the famous MacCrimmon's College of Piping on the Isle of Skye. An honor and well worth it, lass.

"The MacCrimmons, pipers to the MacLeod clan, could be called the greatest Scots pipers ever. They evolved piping to a high art. *Seol Mor* or *pibroch*, it's called. Strictest rules to make the Big Music.

"Uncle Peter mastered it. His music could stir the soul of any Scot. Our mither said his pipe playin' lifted her heart to heaven every time she heard it.

Then, since Firth showed interest early, Uncle Peter taught him the pipes. Passed on all he knew and insisted Firth practice hours each day. Mither sent him up the hill there, mostly. Until my brother got good at it, his music sounded like wailin' banshees."

"Em, was there anything Firth didn't do?" I wiped the sweat off my forehead, and moved over to weed between another garden row.

She sighed. "As I said, Firth was good at all the arts. Came natural.

"And for the pipes he had the natural sense of timin', the far-memory and fey, deep emotions for it. Aye, a wonder he was, and by the time he went off to be an architect, he'd become known and accepted as the New Lauder piper."

Then it hit me. "Your brother? Could he be the piper I saw?" A chill darted up along my spine. "Em, could Firth be a *ghost?*"

The idea terrified me. Had I been lured out of bed in the middle of the night by a ghost? Maybe Em didn't mind ghosties and beasties and things that went bump in the night, but *I* sure did! "Could he be *haunting* us? Mikey and me?"

I stood and shakily brushed bits of weed and moist dirt from my hands. Only moments before I'd been hot and sweaty from the sun, but as I stood there, I felt *cold* and sweaty. The sweat on my face, arms, and the center of my back prickled.

"Em?" I whispered, "am I right? Have you ever...seen him?"

Up until now I hadn't really believed in ghosts. Actually, I hadn't thought enough about the idea to say I believed they could exist or not. Now, suddenly, it seemed easy to believe because I'd seen one. It *had* to be the answer.

Em wore an old brown felt hat to shield her eyes from the sun, but when she looked up at me, nothing could shield the strange, almost stern look in her eyes. "Firth in *any* form is welcome here," she said. "If he chooses to come, if he chooses to stay, this is his home, Christie."

"But he's dead." I stared down at her, understanding now why Castle Lauder and Em had made me feel so uneasy the day we arrived.

"You knew? When I told you about my dream that first time, you knew it wasn't a dream? And the other day? You didn't tell me then, either."

She made that clucking sound with her tongue. "Calm yourself, lass, nothing substantial to tell. If Firth *is* here, I'm the last to see or hear him. Truth is, I've heard it from others."

I still felt cold even though, overhead, the noon sun shone brightly. "Heard *what*?"

Without getting all the way up, she moved a few feet away from me and began picking green beans from the vine. "Visitors from America some years ago told me of their experience on the hill."

"This hill, right?" I asked. "Lauder Hill?"

"Aye," Em said. "But, unlike you, lass, the American couple thought it wondrous, a rare privilege, even. See, this wife happened to be a Lauder descendent. For her, the pleasure of her first trip to Scotland was the tracing down of her ancestral home. I invited them for tea. Then, before they left, this pleasant woman asked if she and her husband might walk the grounds and climb the hill. 'Aye,' I said, and off they went. I thought I'd seen the last of them, but down they came from the hill, rapped on the door, breathless and full of excitement."

"They saw Firth?"

"How they went on. Details down to the last, glossy auburn curl. They were delighted, sure I'd arranged for the pipin' demonstration as a treat for them. Whsst, hardly.

"Imagine how I felt, lass. The hope rose in me and the tears, though I managed to keep together."

"Oh. This couple didn't see what I saw?"

"They did. As you said, not all mist and cobwebby, but solid and full of life. Handsome, they called him, as handsome he was, if it was Firth up there. But they heard him sing and play and they'd listened to every note, enthralled.

"They thought him real as you thought him. So I dinna suppose I knew what to think then. True enough, I dinna ken what to think now. Let's wait for Ian, consult on it with an expert."

"I can describe him," I said, "you would know if—"

She held up a hand. "Hold on, Christie, I ask ye t' wait. When you told me your dream, the hope and the sorrow came floodin' back.

"If t'is true that my dear brother is a haunt, I'd like to ready my mind proper. But don't let's suppose, Christie. Could be the piper is solid and ordinary, as you wondered, a young lad from nearby."

"Could be, I guess," I said. "Em, one thing I'd like to know. When you told Mikey and me those ghost stories, about the Green Ladies and Headless Knights, you didn't seem bothered."

She smiled at me sadly. "You'd know why, if you

think about it, sweet girl. One thing to talk freely of ghosties and beasties and banshees if they're not related. But the ones of our family we've loved and lost and grieved over—"

I interrupted quickly to say, "I ken." And I did ken and sympathized. I knew exactly what Em Lauder meant.

Still, as the day passed, I thought about bedtime and dreaded it. Who knew, I worried, what would happen next?

✤ nine ✤

THE NEXT AFTERNOON EM ushered Dr. Dalvercroft into the kitchen, where I waited.

"Hello, Christie Malcolm," he greeted me, "a pleasure to meet you. I understand you have questions? I'm not certain I can answer them, but I shall try."

"Thank you," I said faintly. Dr. Dalvercroft reminded me in a few ways of my father, mostly his tallness, sandy-colored hair, bushy mustache, and freckles. Of course, Daddy was—had been—about twenty years younger.

He seated himself opposite me at the kitchen table. "Now, what's this all about?" He grinned. "Such a cryptic message, Em, how could I resist?"

Em and I had set the table for tea. On a plate were her still-warm shortbread cookies. He sighed with pleasure as he picked up a cookie. "Big questions and these—both incentives to get me here in a hurry."

Mom and Mikey weren't due back for a couple of hours. If I were lucky, I could find out all I needed to know before Mom returned. If I were extra lucky, the doctor would be long gone before she returned.

It wasn't that I wanted to be sneaky. What could be wrong, I wondered, with learning more about a subject that interested me? Besides, I wanted so much to help Mikey. Of course, I didn't want to force my little brother to remember stuff about a past life as Firth Lauder if it couldn't be true, but—

"First, tea," Em said solemnly, as she moved from the stove to the table with the round white teapot. When she'd seated herself, she nodded at me.

"Let me get us started, lass. Now, Ian, Christie does have questions and I do as well. T'is a matter of concern to me and my long-departed brother. Christie's small brother, Mikey, claims to have lived here before. You're the likely person for us to consult, I thought, since you and I have had some fascinatin' discussions about subjects beyond the ken of the ordinary."

Em leaned forward across the table. "Y'see, the lad Mikey insists that he was *my* dear brother, Firth!"

The doctor's pale blue eyes widened behind his glasses. He turned his gaze toward me. "How old is your brother?"

"Mikey just turned five in June—June eighteenth," I told him, "and Dr. Dalvercroft—"

"Call me Dr. Ian, saves time and voice," he said. "Go on."

"Dr. Ian, June eighteenth is the same day Em's brother got hanged! There's more and I've written it down in my journal."

From the pocket of his shirt he withdrew a small notebook and pen. "I'll take a few notes, if you don't mind," he said. "Now, Christie, tell me from the beginning. What is the first inkling you had that the lad—"

"Wait, I just thought of something." He sat up straighter. "Em, your brother Firth was hanged, and, lass, your brother has asthma.

"Without leapin' to any swift conclusions, the asthma *could be* the...what is called...a *birthmark*. A carry-over mark from one lifetime to the next. Only a suggestion, mind you."

"Birthmark? Dr. Ian, do you really believe in *next* lifetimes?"

"Let's say I believe in keeping my mind open to all possibilities. The idea that we have many lifetimes is not a new idea, you know. It is an ancient and persistent theory, one that many cultures have always considered valid."

"*Reincarnation,* you mean? How does it work, exactly?"

"For now, Christie, why don't you tell me about your brother. His behavior, what he's said, and all of that. He's not here? I would very much like to speak with the lad."

"Sure, maybe." I sighed. "My mother isn't too crazy about the idea, to be honest. She doesn't think it—reincarnation—is true. And she thinks encouraging Mikey would be bad for him. But, Dr. Ian, I don't know how my brother could've known—"

Em reached across the table to pat my hand. "Calm yourself, dearie. Questions are allowed, you know."

I took a deep breath. "You're right, that's what *I* think, too. And I really want to help Mikey.

"Well, anyway, it began the day we got to Scotland, driving from Edinburgh here to the Borders. Mikey told me in the car he lived here once, that he was big, as big as...as a man. He said his name used to be Firth. I didn't understand, I thought he'd said his name was *First.* But then, later, Em told us her brother's name was *Firth.*"

I paused for breath, took a sip of tea, and glanced at Em. She nodded for me to continue.

"Mikey started yelling. He told my mother she had to turn at this road, I mean, lane. He insisted on seeing *his* castle. Then, when Mom drove down the lane, we saw this place...Castle Lauder.

"When Mikey got out of the car and walked closer, he started crying and shaking and talking about a tree up on the hill. I didn't see any tree, but he got so upset, he went straight into one of the worst asthma attacks he's ever had. I thought...I was afraid he would die. That's when Em came out, when she phoned you.

"Dr. Ian, do you think his asthma actually could have come from being...hanged? As Firth, I mean, in a past life?" I looked at him. *"Could it be?"*

The doctor put down his pen and picked up another cookie. "Could it be?" He smiled. "In my opinion?" He gazed at the cookie, took a nibble, then placed it carefully on his plate.

"Yes," I urged. "Tell me."

"Over the years, as a medical doctor and as a psychiatrist, I've come across many ailments for which I could not discover any apparent cause or cure. Frustrating for my patients, frustrating for me as well.

"But, lass, that frustration forced me to widen my mind with a great deal of research. Eventually I came to the conclusion that all those puzzling ailments *did* have a cause—only not from the current life, but an earlier one. Many of the conditions cleared up once the patients understood and could release them."

The doctor smiled. "I came to the idea of reincarnation with many doubts, Christie. I'd been trained as a man of science and was as skeptical as they come.

But after I'd delved into all the ancient texts and literature on the subject of reincarnation..."

He grabbed up the cookie, took a big bite, then another. I pretended to smile, although, at that moment, he reminded me even more of my father.

"In time, after all my reading and interviewing of patients and others during my travels, I thought—"

"I ask you, Em—Christie? Is it truly any more surprising to be born many times as it is to be born once?"

I stared at him. Along with his questions, a wonderful new thought occurred to me. If a person who died would, eventually, be born all over again, then my father could have another chance to live...even, many more chances. Oh, maybe I'd never know or be with him again during my life, but Daddy would start all over, as a baby. I tried to imagine my father as an infant, and I couldn't help but smile.

"Hmmm, I'll have to think about that," I answered Dr. Ian.

"T'is the same in nature, as I told you, Christie." Em spoke up. "In Scotland summer has a short lease. Already I can see the familiar dyin' signs on my plants and on the moor.

"But, always, after the winter, when spring returns, the plants and flowers and trees are born again. The animals are born anew. From the dying comes life again. That's nature telling us what we need to know. Life in all its glory happens, not once, but again and again, generation after generation."

"Well said, Em." He nodded. "Nature sets the patterns out for all to see. Today's science knows that all life is energy—energy patterns. Energy can never be destroyed, only transformed. So, what should we say,

Christie? Death is only a phase in the process we call life. A change, but not the final ending."

I thought for a moment. "You mean the way water changes to snow or rain or ice? Like it doesn't really disappear, just turns into something else?"

"Exactly!" he said. "Now many adults do claim to have memories. But what became intriguing to me, and what I've come to believe is much more reliable are the past-life memories of children. They haven't had the vast exposure to books, movies, history lessons, or sundry other influences, as adults have had.

"Children between the ages of three and five who claim to remember a past life, that's what my interest is. Not my only interest, mind you. I have a number of other specialties that I pursue at the university."

"You know other little kids who remember—like Mikey?" I found it hard to believe.

"Some," Dr. Ian answered. "Other researchers have documented hundreds of such children's cases, mostly in Asia and India. In those countries, reincarnation—the concept of more lives than one—is accepted and always has been.

"My own research takes me to India—where I've just been—and to other countries as well, including the United States."

More lives than one—he said the words easily, I thought.

"Dr. Ian, when Mikey said he lived here when he was bigger, and he told me his name, it scared me. I wanted to believe he was only playing a game, making it up. I got...spooked, I guess.

"My mom got nervous, too, but then she turned around the next day and told me it was only Mikey's imagination working overtime. She can't stand the idea of her little boy as someone else!

"My mother told me and Em not to talk about it anymore with Mikey."

"Would you like me to talk with your mother? Not to convince her of anything, but to explain that Mikey is far from the only small boy or girl with disturbing memories. She might not object as much if she knows the kind of serious research going on in this area."

I shook my head. "Dr. Ian, I don't think my mother *wants* to know. She thinks Mikey just saw a video or television show which, as she said, 'put ideas in his head.' She told me, 'We live, we die, and that's it, period. Anything else is wishful thinking.' She won't talk about it with me."

"I will come by again to meet your mother and brother. If the lad does say or do anything unusual, let me know. Better still, do as you've done—record it in your journal."

"Would you—I mean, tell me again what you said about a birthmark."

"Ah, yes," he said. "In more recent times, when hospital or autopsy reports can be located, a past-life death wound corresponds to a remarkably similar mark or stain on the present-day child or person who claims that kind of violent death happened to him or her. Such a mole or strawberry mark or other physical symptom cannot be considered proof, but a clue.

"In India and Asia, most parents deeply dislike the possibility of having a child who remembers such a violent death. They consider it bad luck and a burden for the child. Not to mention if the child recalls being a murderer!

"Not many families in any culture would like having such a one in the cradle."

Across the table from me, Em made a noise in her throat. "Dinna ye remember, Ian? My brother may have been hanged by vigilantes for thievery and murder, but he was innocent. I always believed it, and Mikey verifies it."

'That's right, doctor," I said. "Mikey keeps insisting he didn't commit the crimes."

"'Tis would explain why he returned," Em added. "He came back to prove his innocence."

"Maybe, Em," I said doubtfully, "but how would Mikey know he'd ever have the chance to travel to Scotland? To the Borders, to this very castle, to *you*, Em?"

"Ye have me there, lass."

"Another thing, Dr. Ian. How come I don't remember any past life?"

"For most children," he said, "those who died a normal death—what is called the 'veil of forgetfulness' in the old books—covers up memories of past lives. This forgetfulness or 'veil' frees the newly born soul to concentrate fully on the present life. Nature knows best, in other words. But for those children who do remember an unnatural or violent death, life is more difficult. It can be traumatic and painful. Those memories may cause health problems or birth defects or marks, carry-overs from the previous life experience."

He sat back. "Do you want to hear more?"

"Oh, definitely. I've never heard of this...never even thought of stuff like this. But it's...I need to know."

"Go on, Ian. Fascinatin'," Em added.

"Another aspect," he continued, "if rebirth is true, is the idea that each of us comes back to learn and to refine ourselves. It suggests that we carry forward into each new life, experience from the past, all that we've ever learned. So, it's possible your brother might express or show signs of abilities he developed during other lifetimes. Now, then, does he have any particular skills or talents or—"

"Aye, I can say it!" Em's eyes brightened. "Firth was a talented artist—sketches and watercolors and, a few times, oils. Sad to say, I've had to sell off a number of his best works to survive these years."

"Not the armoire, Em. Dr. Ian could look at the 'wee faces,' couldn't he?"

"Aye, he could." She patted my hand. "I'd not thought of it. The point is, Mikey also loves to draw and color. He's talented, about the same as Firth was at five. I was too young to recall, but my mither often bragged about it."

Her voice quavered. "Musical too, Firth was. A fine, trained piper. A singer as well. Our pride and joy."

"Mikey adores music, " I said, "but he doesn't even try to sing."

"Christie, has Mikey ever made any claim to being another person before coming to Scotland?"

"Not that I can think of," I answered. "He's such a quiet little guy—wait a minute!—I do remember something."

He poised his pen above a fresh page of his little black book.

"Well, this past winter, right after my—our father died of a heart attack, it snowed a lot. To keep Mikey busy, you know, to take his mind off what was happening, the funeral and all that, I bundled him up and took him outside.

"Behind our house is a hill, too—not as rocky or as steep as this one. But I remember now how Mikey cried. He wouldn't let me zip up his snowsuit all the way, and he totally refused to let me put on his red wool muffler. So I wore it myself.

"Anyway, I wanted to build him a snowman halfway up the hill. I thought it would be fun for him. Instead, he cried and carried on so much, I gave up, and built the snowman for myself. When I put the red scarf around the snowman's neck, you know how you do, he really freaked out.

"I remember how he screamed. Come to think of it, the only other time he screamed and acted like that is the day we came here.

"Now that I think of it, Mikey's always had lots of nightmares. My parents called them 'night terrors.' They said every kid has them and that I had them, too.

"And Mikey would always give me a hard time at bathtime. A hard time when it came time to wash his...neck!"

I felt a chill as I recalled the many times he'd begged me not to touch his neck, and how I'd washed it anyway, fussing at him, not understanding.

"Otherwise," I said, "Mikey's a quiet, sweet little guy. He told me why he didn't want his neck washed— 'It hurts.' No matter how gentle I was about it, he cried and cried and said it hurt him.

"If it turns out to be true, if he was Firth, if he was hanged—"

"*Christie! What are you talking about? What's going on here?*"

Mom stood in the doorway, her face flushed pink with anger. "I thought I told you that subject matter was off limits."

Dr. Dalvercroft rose from his chair. "Mrs. Malcolm—"

Mikey appeared in the doorway with Malkin in his arms. "Hi," he said softly. "Malkin missed me again."

Dr. Ian introduced himself and mentioned that he'd been the doctor Em phoned when Mikey had his attack.

"I owe you thanks then," Mom said stiffly. "My son's recovered nicely. So far." She gave me a look.

"When I walked in just now, you were discussing this past-life business with my daughter?"

Dr. Ian nodded. "I was, aye."

"Nothing against you, Dr. Dalvercroft," Mom said, "but as I told my Christie and Em, I don't think it's in his best interests to encourage Michael's fantasy."

"We were discussing reincarnation, Mrs. Malcolm. Not proven, perhaps, but not exactly considered the realm of fantasy."

My mother rolled her eyes.

"Maybe, just maybe, Doctor, my son's memory is genetic. The children's father, my late husband, was Scots."

Em held up the teapot. "Julia?"

For another few seconds, my mother resisted her invitation to join us, then gave in. She sat down and gave a deep sigh. "Reincarnation is just a theory, Doctor, not proven, isn't that what you said a moment ago? How *can* it be? Who's ever returned from the dead to tell us differently?"

"Ah, you'd be surprised," the doctor said calmly.

"Thanks to the growing numbers of people coming forward to report near-death experiences, we're learning much about what death is and is not."

Dr. Ian's eyes sparkled. I had the feeling he enjoyed debating the subject with my skeptical mother.

"What's *near-death*?" Mikey asked quietly.

"*See?*" Mom looked upset again. "Please, Doctor, if you don't mind, I prefer not to discuss the subject any longer. I don't think it's good for either of my children. Or, for that matter, *me!* Even talking about it could build false hopes. If you ask me, even though I'm not a doctor, I believe it's far healthier to face the fact—dead is *dead!*"

"I could mention," Dr. Ian said pleasantly, "that your genetic memory explanation doesn't explain the many cases where young children recall and give impressive evidence for a lifetime as a member of another race or culture.

"I'd like to at least show you some case histories of other young children who recall past lives. *If* you'd care to read them. Fascinating, I promise, Mrs. Malcolm. It wouldn't hurt to consider the possibilities. Your Mikey's case reminds me of—"

"My son is *not* a case, Dr. Dalvercroft."

I waited for Mom to give him a good example of her temper, but she surprised me. Not very graciously, she shrugged. "Oh, I suppose so. I'm not against reading your material. Anyway, I have a feeling you—all three of you—will probably just keep ganging up on me, if I don't. But if you expect me to believe, don't hold your breath—oh, God!"

She flopped back hard against the chair back. "Is that what you were talking about when I walked in? I just realized—your brother was hanged, Em, and Mikey has asthma. I never put those together. Do you think—"

"For the record, Mrs. Malcolm, I was once as skeptical as you. More so, since my field is medicine …science. I cannot say what I think about what your son has said and done since you came to stay with Em. I *will* say I would like to pursue the matter, if you feel so inclined. Ring me up if you care to visit me at the university. I'd especially enjoy talking with this fine lad."

Mom looked at Em, then back at Dr. Ian. "You're at *what* university?"

"Edinburgh. Parapsychology. Head of the department."

"Parapsychology. Hmmm." My mother smiled. "Imagine that. I guess I'm behind the times."

"Dr. Ian holds the chair at the university."

She stared in my direction, then ran both hands through her already windblown hair. "I give up," she said, "this *is* the twilight zone."

✦ ten ✦

"SWEETIE, WE HAVE TO talk."

"Don't call me that," I snapped.

An expression of hurt confusion spread across my mother's face. "*Sweetie?* Since when have you had a problem with that? You've always been my sweetie, Christie. I've called you that ever since I can remember. What's wrong?"

I'd spoken without thinking. The last thing I wanted was a showdown with my mother. If only I could take my words back, turn this awkward moment around, pretend I'd only been teasing.

But it was too late to cover up. My resentment had slipped through the cracks of the wall I'd built around it.

"Sorry, Mom, but I haven't felt much like a sweetie for a long time. Not since Daddy died. Or for a long time before."

Four days had passed since our visit with Dr. Ian. Since then Mom and I hadn't said much to each other. Now we were alone in the parlor. Mikey had been asleep for hours. Em had gone up to bed earlier than usual. I'd promised her I would bank the fire in the hearth before I went up to bed.

For the past hour or so, Mom and I had sat in separate chairs, each of us reading, the only sounds the crackle of the fire, and the whine and wail of the wind outside.

"Oh, Christie, you never said anything. I thought...well, you seemed to be handling it all so well."

I knew she didn't want me to have any problems. It was easier for her to think I didn't.

"I'm okay, really," I said without looking at her. "Don't worry about it. Anyway, what did you want to talk about?"

She looked very relieved. "Lots of things, Christie. First, though, I want to ask your opinion."

Across the table which separated our chairs, Mom handed me a sheaf of watercolor sketches. "These are my best, so far. Check out the one on top.

"It's a rather simple plaid. The few red threads, the black, with the green and blue predominant. I've softened the colors, but otherwise, I stayed close to the original pattern. Like it?"

"I do like it," I said, "but will you give Mikey credit? That's *his* design."

"Mikey designed a tartan? I can't believe it!"

"Believe it, Mom." I handed the sketches to her and stood up. "It's upstairs, wait, I'll get it."

I found the folded-into-four crayon sketch I'd removed from my jeans pocket and put in the nightstand drawer. Unfolding it in the lamplight, I saw that I'd remembered correctly. The lines of color were exactly the same as Mom's drawing.

When I brought it downstairs to show her, she gasped. "You're right!" She sat back down in the chair and flopped back against the pillows. "I guess I can't pretend something isn't going on. Christie, I intended this particular design—my version of it—as a surprise for Em.

"I discovered a copy of a very old volume of tartans. In it I found one for the Lauder family. Except for the color tones, that's what my sketch is—the Lauder tartan!

Agitated, Mom raked her fingers through her hair. "Now—Mikey's design. Sweetie—Christie—my heart is absolutely pounding. How did he know?"

"That's what I'm telling you," I said. "Mikey had to have been here before. What other explanation can there be except a past life as Firth Lauder?" I asked.

"Not necessarily reincarnation." Mom sighed. "I've thought it could be a case of ESP—extra-sensory perception. Everyone is perceptive," she explained, "or call it *intuitive*, whether we use our abilities or not. And little kids Mikey's age are so open. All of his intuitions began when we reached the Borders. He opened up and tuned in, almost like a radio station can be tuned in."

"Mom," I said, "you heard Dr. Ian say there are plenty of case histories of kids who remember past lives and deaths. Even if you haven't read them yet, don't you really think it has to be more than ESP or intuition?"

I almost felt sorry for her. She obviously still couldn't handle the idea that Mikey might've been a complete other person before he was born to her.

"There's a lot you don't know, Mom. While you've been off working, Mikey's said things, and I've found out *incredible* things that match up to his story."

Since my mother continued to show interest, I told her of Mikey's dread of the tree, and what he'd said about the boulder. I also told her what he had said about being a ghost, briefly, before he flew off to his "big bright light."

"I think what all this means is we're supposed to help them," I said. "Mikey and Em and, yes, Firth— that part of him that's still trapped on Lauder Hill. Mom, please change your mind and let Dr. Ian talk with Mikey.

"Maybe none of this is true, but it *could* be! We can't leave Scotland without finding out, one way or another, can we, Mom? Besides, I just know Mikey could be healthy again if—"

I paused, not sure how much more I should tell her. I decided to keep quiet about what I intended to do, for Mikey's sake.

She didn't answer right away.

"I don't know about you," I said, "but I have to know! I can't sleep as it is. If I don't figure all of this out, I'll probably never sleep at night again in my life!"

"You're not sleeping?"

"No. Not very well, at least. I lie there and think about Daddy and...death. About what it all means, how it works...and why!"

"Oh, Christie," she said softly, "that's what I've been afraid of. I'm afraid both you and your brother are clutching at this idea of reincarnation because of your father's death. I told you before, wishful thinking can be dangerous.

"Oh, not that I wouldn't like to believe it. I would. If death isn't the abrupt, senseless, random event most of us are taught to believe, it would be great. It would make a huge difference in how we lived our lives. But, Christie, it's so speculative, and so far, not proven, not true and—"

"Mom, never mind *true,* for now. All I'm asking is, let Mikey talk with Dr. Dalvercroft. And me, too. I still have questions and things to figure out."

"What kind of questions? What's left to ask? Haven't you heard enough?"

"No."

She gazed down at Mikey's crayon drawing. "All right," she said softly, "you and Mikey have my permission. Before we leave Scotland, we'll spend a few days in Edinburgh. You can call him first, make an appointment. Except you have to promise me, Christie, no matter what more you learn, you must remember something very important."

"What?"

"No matter how fascinating you think all this is, remember, sweetie, today—this minute—is what really counts. What you are, what your brother is *now,* is what's important. Just don't get so lost in the past, that you forget the present, okay?"

She smiled. "Here, listen to this. I read it somewhere. 'The past is history, the future is a mystery, and this moment is a gift. That's why now—this moment— is called *the present.*'"

"Pretty good, Mom. Okay," I agreed. "But here's another thing you don't know yet. You might not think it's important, but I do, and Em does. Listen, the date Firth Lauder got hanged? Mom—Are you ready for this? June eighteenth!"

"Mikey's birthday!"

"Exactly! Now that's strange, right, Mom?"

"Yes," she admitted.

"I know more than half a century has gone by between those two June eighteenths," I said, encouraged, "but—the exact date! It *has* to mean something."

I'd watched her face as I spoke. One instant her expression was stubborn, the next instant, soft and wistful.

"Mom, Em said her brother left life by one door, and Mikey came into life through the same door."

"One door closes, another one opens," she murmured. "I've never heard it's the *same* door, Christie. Now is what matters. The past, whatever it happened to be, is over!"

My mother rose from her chair. She yawned and stretched. "Let's not talk about it anymore tonight," she said. "My brain is sore. I'm ready for bed, are you?"

She waited until I'd fixed the fire, then she turned off the lamps. In silence, side by side, we climbed the stone steps.

"Don't lie awake and worry all night," she said, hugging me. "Have sweet dreams instead...sweetie!"

"'Night, Mom," I answered. "I'll try."

When she'd said, *dreams,* an image of the Piper entered my mind as if he'd pulled back a misty curtain and stepped forward to let me see him.

As I closed the tower-room door behind me, I couldn't help but wonder, and smile to myself. What would Mom say or do if I told her about *him?*

Get dressed for a dream? Never would I have imagined I'd do such a thing. Weird or not, that's exactly what I did as I slipped into my nightgown and put on my robe and fuzzy white slippers.

Even though the air outside was chilly and damp and the wind blew hard, I walked over and pushed open both sides of the window. If Firth played the pipes during the night, I didn't want to chance not hearing the music.

One other thing I remembered to do. After testing to see if the batteries were still fresh, if my little cassette recorder still worked, I slipped it into my robe pocket. If I did find myself on Lauder Hill during the night, I would get the music on tape. No one, not even Mom would argue that kind of evidence, I thought.

Yet after I'd turned out the light, and discovered how hard it was to get comfortable with the recorder in my pocket, I did feel foolish. Still, I didn't change my mind. I simply settled myself flat on my back on top of the covers, closed my eyes, and waited for the usual, sad thoughts about Daddy to take over my mind.

The sad thoughts never arrived. Instead—quickly!— the music came. The pipes' sweet droning notes were distinct above the mournful cries of the night wind.

I sat up in bed, alert, wide-awake and eager. I felt rested, as if I might have already slept for hours.

Excited, I left the bed to rush to the open window. After I'd peered into the foggy darkness for a minute or two, my eyes adjusted and—I saw him!

It seemed to take forever to tiptoe from my room, down the darkened stairs, through the shadowy front hall and the parlor, to the kitchen, through the door onto the tiny back porch. There, I stopped to slip my pair of green rubber Wellies on over my slippers.

The next thing I knew—I didn't remember leaving the castle, or crossing the garden—I'd climbed more than halfway up the hill.

At my back I felt that strong force again, a force which spun me forward up along the rocky path. Faster and faster I moved upward—I pinched the skin on the back of my hand to make sure I was awake. I *felt* awake, I *had* to be.

Still…I doubted it, too. It had to be a dream. Otherwise, how else could I explain the mysterious, amazing force that moved me?

Ahead, just out of reach, the mist had formed into criss-crossed white ribbons. Neat, intersecting lines, some narrow, some wide. And, faintly, I made out colors threaded through the white mist, stripes of red, green, blue, black!

How could it be? Spread like a length of cloth above me in the air—a pattern I recognized. The Lauder tartan!

From behind the mist-drawn plaid, I heard the pipes. I stood absolutely still to listen.

It occurred to me then. I had a way to test whether the music existed, or if I only dreamed it. I reached down into my robe pocket. If ever I'd really needed the mini-recorder, the time was now!

The music stopped. I felt another push at my back, and this time I found myself at the top of the hill. All around me the colorful ribbons of mist wove and rewove the same plaid pattern.

Except for the swirling movements of the mist, I couldn't see a thing. It was so quiet. Too quiet, I decided uneasily. It was as if I'd walked into a snowbank, so that even tiny sounds—wind, rustlings of leaves—had been muffled.

I waited for the pipe music to begin again.

"Hello? Piper? Firth?"

As soon as my words were out of my mouth, I felt like a fool. Only for a few seconds, though. I reasoned that since the Piper, if he really was Firth Lauder, could play the bagpipes and sing, he could talk to me.

Nothing. No sound. I began to feel nervous as I watched the mist. If Firth hadn't gone, he would stand somewhere just inside the patterned mist.

I didn't move. I knew if I took one wrong step I might tumble over the craggy ledge.

But when the mist thinned to almost nothing and I could see again, where I'd been sure the piper stood, at the very edge of the highest peak, was only a dark, empty space. He had gone.

Disappointed, I turned slowly and started down the path. By the faint light of the moon, I picked my way, fighting what felt like a strong breeze. I knew it had to be the same strange force that had made the climb up the hill so easy.

A sudden skreel of pipes close by made me nearly jump out of my skin. I turned my head toward the sound.

"Oh!" On the big, flat rock at the side of the path—Mikey's rock—the Piper sat playing softly. He seemed totally unaware of me standing near. I could see that the misty ribbons had formed above and around him. From where I stood I could see how fast the mist closed like a cocoon around him.

I remembered how the mist had muffled every sound. I guessed it was why he hadn't looked up when I'd cried out.

Even in the dark, I could see him well enough. He looked so alive! His teeth and the whites of his eyes caught and reflected the moon's silvery gleam. His wavy dark hair blew gently in the breeze, as real hair would. *Could* he be a ghost? I wondered. It didn't seem possible. Still—

"Who are you?" I called. "Tell me your name, please."

He didn't even look up. Instead, he'd begun to play the pipes louder, with more attention to what he was doing. I didn't know this tune.

I looked down at my own hands, pale and ghostly in the moonlight. I called to him again, louder. His chin lifted and he appeared to be looking in my direction, but I could tell as he blew into the chanters, that he didn't know I was there.

If he wouldn't talk, I could at least tape-record his music. I pushed down the button on the mini-recorder and held it out toward him.

Almost as if he wanted to cooperate, he began to sing.

> *In the gloaming, oh, my darling,*
> *when the lights are dim and low...*
> *will you think of me and love me,*
> *as you did once long ago...*

As he sang, I felt a lump in my throat and the sting of tears behind my eyelids. I didn't want to cry, not here. But when his song ended, I couldn't help it. I sobbed and sobbed. I just stood there in the misty dark night and let all my sad, scared, hopeless feelings pour out.

Through my tears I could see the Piper, but I knew, even as I cried, that he couldn't see me, and never would. What I knew about him at that moment made me cry all the harder. Yet, the knowledge that came to me—the answer—made me feel better at the same time.

I knew what the Piper was. He was not Firth, or, at least, not all of what Firth had been when he'd lived. No, this piper I saw seated on the rock was only a fragment of Firth Lauder, a trapped piece of the young man he'd once been. The piper I saw and heard played his songs over and over, couldn't escape this scene of his death. He could play and sing and exist in the same pattern ...

I'd been sobbing for myself, but I stopped as I realized how lucky I was to be alive. Poor, poor Firth, I thought, and as I did, another realization hit me. I knew then, exactly what I could do to help Mikey get well and strong again. At the same time I could help Em regain her family's belongings.

If Firth could get free from repeating over and over his tragic death...

Only one thought stopped me. To free the ghost of Firth Lauder, I would have to get Mikey involved. I would need his help. Yet I could be taking a huge risk, I thought. The risk could be a matter of life or death.

Not my life or death, but Mikey's.

I continued down along the path in the semidark. My tears stopped, but my heart was thudding hard in my chest.

By the time I'd reached the foot of Lauder Hill, I knew I'd have to chance it.

It'll be worth it for everyone if it works, I told myself as I headed across the wet grass toward the castle.

If...

✤ eleven ✤

"EM, DOES THE WORD *broch* mean anything to you? I mean, *is* it even a word?"

"*Broch?* Why brochs stand about all over Scotland. Built way back in Roman times, or, more likely, ancient Pictish times. Brochs are thought to be watchtowers or wee forts.

"Hav'na you seen them, lass? Up Lauder Hill, beyond on the moor, are several of those small stone brochs or *cairns* as they're called, too.

"Firth and me, we imagined they were auld gray thumbs of giants. We played hide-and-seek in them or pretended to be warriors in battle."

As I listened to her explanation, I felt more certain that I was on the right track. On my first climb up the hill with Mikey, I *had* glimpsed a couple of those stone thumbs rising up from the heather and rough grass.

I knew then I would have to get started as soon as possible to do what I had to do with Mikey. *Soon* meaning *today*, I thought. That is, if I can just work up enough courage ...

Earlier I'd awakened to see the mini-recorder beside me in bed. Memories of my experience with Firth's ghost flooded my brain. I sat up, excited at the prospect of having caught his music, his 'In the Gloaming' song on tape.

Right away, I rewound the tape, then pushed down the play-back button. If I have the proof on tape, I decided, I can—

Instead what played back to me were only eerie whooshes, whines, and whispery noises. I sat back against the pillows, disappointed. No way would I be able to convince anyone that what I'd caught on tape could be bagpipe music or a song. Those weird whines and whispers sounded like wind, nothing else.

But if I didn't have the audio evidence, what I did have was what seemed to be an important clue. Important because of the powerful image that appeared in my mind as I lay back against the pillows. A clear image and a word, or what I hoped would be a word, although I couldn't remember ever hearing it before.

Into my mind came the Piper's face, his expression intense, his mouth forming a word I couldn't hear. The picture I could see so clearly was the way he'd looked the second night I'd seen him.

Over and over I saw his mouth form the single word. I hadn't known what he'd been trying to tell me that night, but I knew now. At first I thought the word was simply *rock*, but, no, I couldn't mistake the shape of his lips as he formed a *B*. Not *rock—broch*.

Now that Em had confirmed for me there was such a word, I knew I had to follow my hunch. *Broch* had to be the clue I needed in order to start. It had to be!

So far, the morning had been gray and drizzly, but through the kitchen window I could see a few rays of brilliant sun break through the clouds. For me the improved weather was one more signal to go forward with my plan.

"Let's go, peanut," I said after breakfast, before Mikey got busy with his crayons or the set of toy knights he'd found on a shelf in his—Firth's—bedroom. "We've been indoors too much. Good morning for a climb up the hill and a walk on the moor."

Mikey didn't need coaxing. I stood by, as he tried, and succeeded in tying his shoelaces by himself. I was proud of him, and myself, too, since I'd been the one to show him how.

I rushed to hug him. "Perfect!" I said. "What a smart guy you are! Now, let's make a picnic lunch to take with us. Would you like that?"

He nodded eagerly. Em also seemed to think a *ramble* (her word for *walk*) was a grand idea. "I'll help make up your picnic. What would ye like? Dinna forget to take jackets, and wear sturdy shoes and trousers against the brambles, lass."

While Em and I made the lunch, I felt close and comfortable with her. Even if I hadn't felt certain we were connected because of Mikey, I'd already begun to think of her as another grandmother, or—simply—a grand friend.

"Would ye like to take along my binoculars?" Em asked as we prepared to leave. "I often use them when I'm gathering herbs or mushrooms or when I'm birding. All sorts of birds up there—grouse, blackcock, pheasant.

"Not that I climb the hill so much anymore." She grinned. "Comes from getting gray and limpy and long in the tooth."

Mikey and I laughed at the horrible witch face she

made at us. "Thanks, Em, I will take the binoculars."

As Mikey and I were about to leave and head for the hill, I nearly changed my mind. I thought about confessing to Em my true reason behind this happy little outing. I felt tense. If something were to happen to Mikey...

I decided against telling her. Why worry her? Or, even if I didn't explain *how* I intended to find her family's lost treasures, why build up her hopes? What I intended, what I hoped would happen, might not.

All during our slow climb up the stony path, I thought about what it would mean if we did uncover the treasures in one of those ancient, skinny stone towers. Not only would I uncover the treasure, but, also, the truth!

Every few minutes, I glanced at Mikey's small form as he trudged ahead of me. If he truly had lived as Firth Lauder in a previous lifetime, I knew, like Em, he'd been innocent. My little brother—so sweet, so good.

"Want a rest, Mikey? We can stop here a while."

He glanced around, saw the tree, and shook his head. I saw fear flash in his eyes.

"Not *here*," he whispered. "Don't like that tree."

"I know you don't now. But you used to like the tree. Em told me it used to be your friend. You climbed it lots of times, didn't you? Why...why don't you try again, Mikey. Make friends with the tree again?"

I absolutely hated to see the frightened rabbit look on his dear little face. His bottom lip quivered, his eyes begged me not to ask it of him. I'd never, never meant him any harm, and I didn't want to scare him now. But I knew I had to make him remember.

Except as I took hold of his hand and led him

across tussocks of grass toward the dark, gruesome-looking tree, I could feel him tremble. "No, don't want to," he whimpered.

"Okay, you don't have to climb it, but you do—we do have to sit under it. It's very important, Mikey. You'll understand some day, but right now, you have to help me. Help Em, too.

"You want to help me and Em, don't you, peanut?"

"I do-o-o-o..."

My heart ached for him. "I know you do, sweetie," I crooned.

After we'd settled ourselves on the rough grass inches away from the dark tree trunk, I let go of Mikey's hand. He tried to move closer to me, but I wouldn't let him.

"H-hold me, Christie," he said. "I'm a-scared."

When I heard him gasp slightly between words, I hesitated. Should I really go on with this? I asked myself. Do I dare? Because I could see his thin little body shake as he sat there, and his breathlessness told me what I'd been afraid would happen, really could happen to him.

If I kept at him, forced him to remember, kept him there beneath this half-dead tree, Mikey definitely could suffer another asthma attack. Could I, as his sister, his second mother, not only let it happen, but deliberately *make* it happen?

I bit my lip hard, then plunged ahead. "When you were big, before you were born to Mommy, what was your name? You told me before, tell me again."

His green eyes were huge with terror. "Don't 'member."

"Yes, you do! *Tell me.* Tell me right this minute, or

I'll get mad. I'll get very, very mad because...listen, it's so important!"

I didn't want to give up, or lose control of myself. But when I saw the hurt and fear in his eyes as I yelled at him, I felt totally ashamed of myself.

"I'm sorry," I cried. "I'm so sorry, I don't want you to be afraid anymore. Mikey, peanut, I just want you to be strong again, I want you to be able to *breathe* again. I want you to be well and free and oh, I want—"

"Firth," Mikey whispered, leaning forward. He said it again in a stronger voice. "Firth...Lauder."

I stared at him. "Okay...who's Calinda, Firth? Remember Calinda? Calinda Douglas? Was she your sweetheart?"

"Aye."

"You loved her?"

"With all my heart and soul," Mikey said in a firm voice.

"You didn't kill her, did you, Firth?" I said. "Do you know who did?"

Afraid to break the spell, I let my questions tumble out fast, one after another. I couldn't believe it; just as I'd hoped, my little brother *could* remember his past life. He could help me help him!

He stared up at the twisted, bare branches above us.

"Calinda...Ca-linda." He repeated her name so tenderly and the expression on his thin little face was so loving, I wasn't prepared for the loud angry cry that burst from his mouth.

Before I could move, Mikey had scrambled to his feet and stood right over me, his green eyes narrowed to slits as he focused on my face. He looked wild... fierce, not like anyone I knew!

"I willna die! I canna!"

My turn to tremble and be afraid, but I took a risk and asked the rest of my questions anyway. "Where should I look? Which broch, Firth? I can help you get free. I promise. You know what really happened. You're the *only* one who does know. Please, you have to tell."

His eyes widened as he stared at me.

"You ken, Firth Lauder. Tell me the hiding place!"

Before I could stop him, Firth—Mikey—took off running. For a few seconds, before I could get myself up off the ground, I panicked. Mikey should *not* run like that, I thought. It was absolutely the worst thing he could do.

I took off after him, barely noticing the binoculars banging against my collarbone as I ran.

As I ran, I saw, far across the sunlit moor, several small stone towers. Mikey headed straight toward them.

I knew he had to be tiring, but he ran so fast, I still hadn't caught up with him.

I watched him run past the first broch, then stagger to a halt at the second in line. He just stood there, his back to me, his head down. I ran faster, afraid of what I would find when I reached his side.

When I came to a stop before the narrow stone tower, I looked at my brother.

He *did* look exhausted, and worse—his chest heaved.

"Dig down...beneath the front...stone," he said in a low halting voice.

When I knelt down and reached out to hold him in my arms, he resisted me at first. "Willna die," he repeated.

"Mikey, it's me—Christie. Mikey, peanut, it's me."

"Willna die," he said again angrily. His small body shook as I held him loosely within the circle of my arms.

I spoke to him in a calm voice, I soothed him as I've always done before by gently rubbing his back and shoulders, by reassuring him. "Take it easy, Mikey. Christie's here."

And for the next few minutes, as quietly and as clearly as I knew how, I explained to him what I believed. I told him that in his last life he'd been Firth, but he was Mikey now. I told him that he'd once been a bagpiper, and, yes, he'd once worn the kilt—the Lauder tartan. Mikey's eyes brightened when I said that.

"You told us, how a long time ago when you were bigger you got hanged from the tree. But that's all over with now, Mikey, and you don't have to stay up on the hill by the tree, or sit on the rock. You don't have to play and sing all those songs anymore. You want to breathe better and grow up to be as big and as strong as our Daddy was?"

"Really big, Christie?"

"You can, you sure can. What you have to do is let Firth know somehow that he's free to leave. Tell him you need his energy back and his good lungs and breath. I bet he'll listen to you, Mikey."

He shook his head. "Don't know how to find him, Christie," he said. He looked scared again, so I stopped talking and just held him until I felt him relax.

Had I done the wrong thing telling Mikey what I thought? I hoped not and I shuddered to think what my mother would say if she could've heard what I said.

Until Mikey looked me in the eye and smiled his sweet, tired, little-boy smile, I didn't dare put him down. At last I set him on the ground. He looked okay to me.

"Look, Mikey, Em will be so-o-o happy you found her family treasures."

After what seemed an hour of steady nail-breaking scratching at the dirt beneath the front stone, my efforts paid off. About six inches into the crumbly black soil, I spotted the glint of tarnished silver. I kept digging until I had unearthed one large tin. Just below it in the dirt, another glint of silver.

Painstakingly, I pried both tins out of the ground, praying the old tarnished silver wouldn't break apart in my hands.

I lifted the cover and saw the top layer of the tin's contents: papers, books, and several carved wooden boxes. Under that top layer, I found a pair of silver candlesticks and a heavy metal box that clinked loudly when I shook it.

In the second tin, under layers of what appeared to be mostly official documents and ledgers, I spotted a small book with a faded red leather cover. On the front cover of the book, in graceful black script was written: *Private—Keep Out: Diary of Calinda Douglas.*

Oh, I couldn't wait to read what this young woman who lived half-a-century ago had to say about her life, and about Firth. I would bring the book to Em but I felt sure she'd let me read it, too.

I carried the lightest of the two tins back to the castle. All the way down the hill Mikey didn't say much and I worried that I'd confused and hurt him.

I kept thinking about Calinda's diary, though.

Would we finally find out who had murdered her, and why?

I knew it couldn't have been Firth Lauder. I *hoped* it hadn't been—for Em's sake and ours—Mikey, Mom and me.

✦ twelve ✦

Diary:
I cannot think what to tell him to make
him go away. He nags at me, glares at me.
This very afternoon he took hold of my shoul-
ders and shook me hard as if I were a rag doll.
The look in his eyes terrified me. He raged: "If
I canna have ye, no one will!"

Only a month before my marriage to Firth
and Rab is crazed. Heaven help me, I'm sore
afraid of him...

Calinda's diary told the whole sad story—the story
of a young woman who hadn't meant any harm, who,
out of temporary boredom and impatience, flirted
with the wrong person. From what she wrote it was
certain that she'd had no hint that Firth's cousin, Rab
Hawlie, could be capable of violence. No, it was clear
to all of us that fun-loving Calinda had played an innocent but dangerous game and lost. She'd lost and so
had Firth.

We all sat around Em's kitchen table—Em, Mom,
Dr. Ian, and me—and took turns reading. The doctor
had been just about to leave for Edinburgh when Em

reached him by phone. "Interested? I'll be right over," he'd told her.

Em and I had waited impatiently for him to come, and for Mom to return from her business. I was relieved when Mikey fell asleep on the parlor couch with Malkin. He'd had a hard enough day as it was, I knew.

Diary:
Rab brought me another bouquet this morning. Along with the flowers, he brought another gift. Diary, when I opened the tiny velvet box and saw the diamond ring inside, I knew I had gone too far.
In his awful eyes I saw passion so fierce I felt sickened. Imagine, he actually wanted me to say I would be his bride, not Firth's.
Dear God, what have I done?

We knew now what she'd done. What Rab Hawlie—Em's and Firth's cousin—had done came out of his secret hate and jealousy of his handsome, talented, well-liked rival, Firth. He couldn't steal Calinda away from his rival as he'd hoped, so he'd murdered her instead. Rab stole from her family and from the Lauders to cover up his crimes and to make it look as if Firth had done the crimes.

Obviously, Em said, it had been Rab who convinced Calinda's brothers that Firth was the guilty one. She shook her head sadly. "Aye, the fourth person in the hanging party had to be my own cousin.

No wonder Rab took such good care of me while he lived," Em said sadly. "A guilty conscience, but to the end of his days he kept up the pretense of goodness.

Why, he was sheriff for twenty years. Poor devil," she added, "what a sorry debt he had to pay. As he sowed in life, so will he reap that same crop in lifetimes to come." Em smiled across the table at Dr. Ian. "Isn't that what you say reincarnation means? What we do in one life follows us into the next?"

"Aye," the doctor said, looking at me, "the law of *karma*, or put in scientific language, the law of cause and effect."

I felt so bad for Calinda, but even worse for Firth Lauder. I knew Em felt deeply relieved that her faith in her brother had been based on the truth. To me, though, I couldn't stop thinking about how sad it all was, for all of them, even Rab Hawlie.

After reading aloud the entire diary, it was clear to me that Calinda had been a nice-enough person. Natural, I thought, that she'd been flattered at first by Rab's devotion and attention. Her mistake had been letting it go too far, leading him on when she didn't really like him. Still, what an awful price to pay.

Em reached over to pat my hand. "Dinna be depressed, lass. Thanks to you and to wee Mikey, I can rest easy now and let the old troubles fall from my back. You've helped to put my mind to rest and make my last days brighter, dearie.

"And," she continued, "I wouldna take up a grudge against Calinda. Would be to my own detriment if I did. I'll think of her as I always have, kindly and with deep affection. She was a wee misguided, but not bad. How she suffered."

I saw my mother brush a tear from her eye. "Such a sad, sad story," she murmured.

We all nodded at each other, in silent agreement.

Still, as Em said, it was good to finally know the truth.

"On a happier note," my mother said, "I've been in touch with Pennington. They insist I spend a couple of days in Edinburgh before we leave Scotland. They've even gotten us tickets to see the famous Edinburgh Tattoo." She looked at me intently. "How does that sound, Christie? A little sightseeing? Some good shopping? A night in a fine hotel?"

"Sounds good to me, Mom," I said and meant it.

"I've also given them my blessing to talk with you, doctor—if you're not too busy."

"I will make time, Mrs. Malcolm. I look forward to the next developments in this fascinating saga." He grinned at me. "Phone me up and we'll get together. In fact, why don't I take you all to lunch while you're there. Come to think of it, I have yet to talk with Mikey. How is he faring through all this?"

"Fine," I answered, but his words sent a strong flash of guilt straight through me.

My mother leaned toward Dr. Ian. "If you're taking us to lunch, would you be sure to make reservations for five. Em's coming to Edinburgh with us, aren't you, Em? As my guest, or," she grinned, "as the guest of Pennington Textiles. I insisted they arrange for an extra ticket for the Tattoo."

I couldn't keep silent another second. "Would someone please tell me, what *tattoo*? I mean, what's the big deal?"

Em exchanged glances with Dr. Ian and they both tried to hide their smiles. "You'll see for yerself soon enough, lass. Expect a treat, that's all I'll tell ye.

"I accept your kind invitation, Julia. I'll be glad to see the grand, gray city again. It's been years since I've had the pleasure." Her eyes lit up. "Aye, and while I'm there, I'll consult with a lawyer to set my affairs in order. Thanks to the safe return of certain documents, I may again know a bit o' prosperity."

The "grand, gray city," she'd called it. As I remembered from my brief time in it, the day we arrived, it seemed a perfect description. "So when are we going, Mom?"

All at once I couldn't wait to get away from Castle Lauder, and the nagging worry that, for all my efforts, I hadn't changed a single thing for the better. Not for Mikey, not for myself either. I wondered how I ever could be sure I had cleared the way for my little brother to be healthier and stronger. I still had lingering doubts. Had I been right about the piper on the hill, or had it all been for nothing?

I felt glad and relieved to leave those worries on the back burner with Em's teakettle on the bright, sunshiny morning when the four of us set off in the rental car for Edinburgh.

Everyone else was excited, and before too long, I was, too. A change of scene would be good for me, I thought, good for us all.

Excitement turned out to be the key word for the grand, gray city. During this last week of August, the city streets, shops, and eating places were mobbed. Every year, I learned, Edinburgh hosted this great international festival. Thousands and thousands of people came to it from all over the world. When we arrived later that morning, and had checked into a beautiful hotel, I could feel the crackle of energy in the air.

So much activity going on around me—people, places, colors, laughter, the rhythm and buzz of foreign languages being spoken. Mikey's eyes got bigger and bigger with every minute that passed, and I imagined my eyes had to be just as wide.

The four of us had lunch at a cute little tea shop that had photos of Queen Elizabeth all over the walls and a sign that boasted that the Queen—"a frequent guest"—preferred the Bide-A-Wee over all other Edinburgh tea shops.

After lunch, Em took Mikey in hand to show him the sights, especially the street performers: mimes, clowns, pipers, magicians, and musicians of all sorts. Mom and I went shopping. We ended up with a bag full of new clothes—for me a gorgeous Fair Isle sweater and tartan skirt. We bought a plaid tam for Mikey and a matching plaid scarf for Em.

That evening after dinner we dressed up and went to the theater. At the Young Lyceum on Cambridge Street we saw "They Shoot Horses, Don't They?" Mikey fell asleep, which was just as well, because the rest of us cried off and on during the entire performance. Afterwards, we all agreed it had been fun to cry —as Em put it, "to let the tears fall where they may."

The next day Em went off to her appointment with the lawyer and came back grinning. "All's well with my world again, dearies," she told us.

I phoned Dr. Ian and we arranged to meet him at noon at our hotel. During lunch, he and Mikey had a chance to talk, one-on-one. But from what I could overhear, my brother had little to say about his past life. I wondered if the doctor was disappointed, but he certainly didn't act like it. He was a perfect host, and the food turned out to be perfect, too. After lunch I declared the fresh salmon—"the food of Kings" as it said on the menu—and raspberry trifle to be my all-time favorite food.

That evening we went to the Tattoo.

The Tattoo turned out to be a sound-and-light show, held on the grounds of the famous, ancient Edinburgh Castle. Em explained it, as we huddled together in our seats on the castle esplanade.

"It's the world's best-loved exhibition. Visitors thrill to it, and we Scots never fail to delight in the massed pipe bands, and marching bands. See if it doesna get yer own Scots blood poundin', lass—the rousing music, splendor, and pageantry."

I didn't have to wait long. With the audience, I gasped and applauded at each performance. Military bands, police bands did precision drills to take my breath away. *Amazing*, had to be the only word to describe it!

What I never expected, and what I know I'll never forget, turned out to be the Tattoo's finale. Em hadn't even hinted at what would happen at the end of the program. I realized afterwards that she hadn't wanted to spoil the surprise, or its special effect on me.

At the end, all the lights on the Esplanade dimmed, then went out. I watched as a single spotlight panned slowly up the ancient castle wall to its highest point.

The spotlight found and shone brightly on a lone figure on the castle parapet. A lone piper!

I gasped when I saw the piper standing in the circle of light.

"Just like the Piper," I whispered to Em, "like your brother or that part of him trapped on the hill. I think…oh, Em, it's still so sad. Firth was the last of the Lauder pipers. Never again will—"

She turned to look at me as if I were crazy. "Why, lass, you're away wi' the fairies if ye think that now. Why, dinna you know, you've made it possible?"

"Made what possible?" I whispered back.

"In time, when your sweet, magical, mystical nightdoings on the hill take hold good and proper, wee Mikey will take on that title."

"Em—you mean?"

"Aye, I mean *your* brother, not mine, is the Lauder piper. And maybe not the last. Remember, Christie, as I told ye, in all of nature, nothing is ever gone forever. I remind you, *my* brother and now *yours* is good at all the arts."

"Oh, I hope," I breathed.

She picked up my hand and warmed it in her own. "Do hope, lass. Keep it always alive in yerself, along with the magic."

For as long as the lone piper paced back and forth on the parapet, piping "Amazing Grace," I let my tears fall freely. If my heart was breaking or mending, I wasn't sure. All I knew, as I watched this lone piper, was that I wouldn't have missed this night—this beautiful sight—for anything in the world.

"He's playing taps," Mom said, looking past Em at me. "A goodbye." Her eyes were bright with tears. "You know who should be here."

I reached across Em's lap to squeeze my mother's hand. "Daddy *is* here, Mom. I can feel him. You know him—he wouldn't have missed this for the world."

I said it to make her feel better, but, the minute the words were out, I knew it was true. As the piper high up on the castle parapet played his final fare-well, I said a silent hello to my father...

Douglas Malcolm, proud descendant of kings.

Not a goodbye, I thought. Hadn't Em said that nothing is ever gone forever? Hadn't I learned that for myself here in Scotland?

When the lights came up again, I looked at the people seated around me. Every one of them was busy brushing tears from their eyes.

Back at the hotel, as I got Mikey ready for bed, he smiled at me sleepily. "I liked the sword dance best, Christie," Mikey said. "Didn't you?"

I hugged him. "Now don't tell me you used to do the sword dance, too."

Mikey stared at me with a puzzled look on his face. "Don't know how yet," he said softly. "I'm only five."

I looked around the hotel room, but I could tell that Mom and Em hadn't heard what Mikey had just said.

I drew in a deep breath and let it out again slowly. I knew what it meant to me. Mikey was not only himself again, my own special little brother, but he was much, much more. He was as Dr. Ian put it at lunch "the sum total of all the lives he'd ever lived."

Funny, I felt more like myself, too—more of a full person than I ever had before. I doubted if I'd be able to explain my feeling to anyone else. Not that I had to. *I* knew what I felt. Instead of trapping all kinds of good energy, blaming Mom for the life I didn't have, now I could be different.

I could be different starting this minute, I decided. And when I left Scotland tomorrow, I had an exciting, still unknown life waiting for me at home.

I looked forward to it and I knew without question I could make it happen.

Hadn't I learned? Anything in life is possible ...